About the Author

It was as a teacher and parent that Rose Impey first started telling her own stories, and they were so well received she soon started writing them down. Rose writes fantastic books for all ages – she wrote the best-selling *Sleepover Club* books for younger readers and the wonderful *My Scary Fairy Godmother* was her first Orchard book for older readers. Rose lives in Leicestershire where, as a young teacher, she inspired a number of budding netball players to believe that if you really care enough you can achieve great things.

For all my original netball team
R.I.

ORCHARD BOOKS
96 Leonard Street, London EC2A 4XD
Hachette Children's Books Australia
Level 17/207 Kent Street, Sydney, 2000, NSW
ISBN 1 84362 560 1
First published in Great Britain in 2005
A paperback original
Text © Rose Impey 2005
The right of Rose Impey to be identified as the
author of this work has been asserted by her in accordance
with the Copyright, Designs and Patents Act, 1988.
A CIP catalogue record for this book is available
from the British Library.
1 3 5 7 9 10 8 6 4 2
Printed in Great Britain

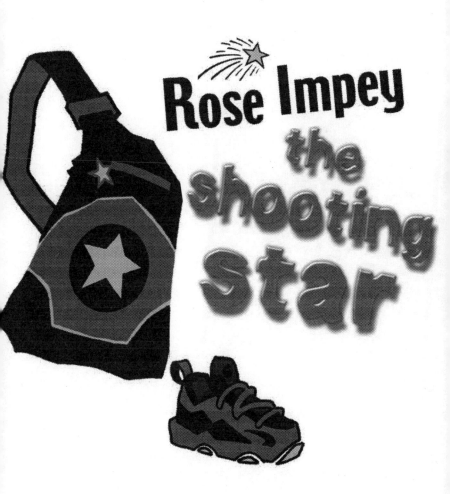

Rose Impey

the shooting star

ORCHARD BOOKS

one

This is the most important day of my life. In a few hours it'll all be over. Not my life! I'm only eleven, for goodness' sake. I mean the finals! To hear the rest of the team singing and cheering at the back of the bus, you'd think we'd already won. But one thing I've learnt over the last couple of weeks is: *don't count your goals till they're in the net.*

I suppose I'd better start at the beginning. That's where stories start, right? Not that I'd know a lot about that 'cos I'm not much of a reader. I don't write at all, if I can help it. And before you ask, I'm rubbish at sums. I bet you're thinking: she sounds like a bit of a loser. Oh, boy, have you got a surprise coming. Like Gav says: there's different ways of being clever. Everyone's got their own little bit of magic inside, it's just a case of finding it – which is what this story's all about.

I *could* start with the bad news and give it to you straight on the chin, just like Miss Summers gave it to us – but you probably need to know a bit about me first, then you'll understand

why it was *such* bad news.

My name's Jelly Jackson. OK, Angelina Jackson. Crap name right! But to be fair, when Mum and Dad chose it they didn't know I'd turn into this five foot seven beanpole with enough frizzy black hair to stuff a cushion. Everyone calls me Jelly, even at home – 'cos I'm a total jelly-freak. My dad reckons that's why I'm always on the go. He says too much sugar makes me hyperactive, but my mum says I was just the same when I was a baby, before I got into eating jelly cubes. She says I just about came out bouncing and I've been bouncing ever since.

I bet I sound a bit gabby, don't I? The funny thing is: I never used to be, before all this netball trouble. Not like Abi, our Goal Defence – now she *is* gabby, *gabby Abi*, you'll see when you meet her. I've never been like that. But when the bombshell came – well, someone had to start making a fuss, didn't they?

The main thing you need to understand is: NETBALL'S MY LIFE! It's all I've ever been good at. You see, with netball, you don't have to be good at things like reading, or sums. Netball's so fast there's no time to stop and think. You just *know* what to do. And you do it. Block, intercept, pass, run, catch, stop, SHOOT! Which is where I come in. They don't call me the *Shooting Star* for nothing. Once I get in the circle, with the ball in my hands – and everyone round me shouting, *'Fly, Jelly, fly!'* – nothing can stop me. I feel like I could actually take off – like a real shooting star. And then I really know there's *something* I'm good at. No, better than good. The best!

So no one, but no one, was gonna take it away from me. Not even Mrs Patsy Poysner, the old toad. Her and her stupid plans to stop us playing netball at school. I mean, how loony is that?

What made it so much worse was: we were this close to winning the cup. Our school has never won any cups before. It must be the only one on the planet where the boys can't even kick a football straight. But now we had this brilliant netball team. All the other schools were scared of us, 'cos word got around that we were seriously, I mean *totally*, unbeatable. It was partly thanks to our teacher, Miss Summers. She's really put some work in on us over the last year. And there we were – tipped to win the county finals – when THE BOMBSHELL came!

It was a couple of weeks ago, at the end of netball practice. We were still out on the playground. Miss Summers likes to do this de-brief thing. We were all wishing she'd get on with it 'cos we were cold and it was starting to rain. Suddenly she looked like she was gonna start crying! She does that sometimes. We're Miss

Summers's first class since she left college and Mum says she hasn't toughened up yet. But we all think she's the best. You could see she'd got something big on her mind, though. Suddenly she came out with it.

'I suppose I'd better give you this straight on the chin,' she said. 'I'm afraid this is our last netball practice – *ever!*

I thought, what's she on about? Has she got some dreadful disease? Is she having a baby? Has she completely lost it? It had gone so quiet you could almost hear our brains working overtime. Zandra's brain worked fastest as usual.

'But what about the final, Miss Summers?' she said.

'Yeah,' said Abi. 'What's gonna happen about the final?'

'I'm afraid...it's been cancelled,' Miss Summers told us.

Well, then all hell broke loose. Everyone was talking at once and at the tops of their voices. When Miss Summers finally managed to quieten us down, she explained, 'From next term the council are banning competitive sports in all county primary schools. There won't be any more netball – not as we know it.'

'Excuse me!' said Maxine, as if her ears were playing tricks on her. 'Banning *netball?*'

'Not just netball. All sports. But there will be

other kinds of er, non-competitive games we can play,' said Miss Summers. 'And we can still have Sports Day. There just won't be any races, as such.'

It was getting crazier by the minute. '*Sports day, without races!* I shouted. 'What kinda screwball thought that one up?'

Hemma nudged me and Zandra tutted a bit. But Miss Summers just smiled. That's what happens when I get mad – it all comes out in a rush. Other teachers look down their noses, like I've made a bad smell or something. But Miss Summers knew I wasn't being rude. Anyway, it was true, it had to be some kind of screwball, didn't it?

'But why are they banning it?' Hemma asked.

'The council members don't agree with competition,' Miss Summers said. 'They want us to work together in school, not against one another. Not everyone can be good at sport, so they don't think it's fair to those who aren't.'

We still didn't get it. 'Sounds barmy,' I said.

Miss Summers gave a big sigh. 'I know, Jelly. And I did try to talk to Mrs Barker about it...'

I knew she would have, even though she's scared of her. Mrs Barker's our headteacher, and believe me her bark's as bad as her bite. My mum's one of the cleaners at our school and she says the other cleaners call Mrs Barker *The-One-Who-*

Must-Be-Obeyed. Not to her face, of course.

'You gotta tell her again,' said Abi. 'You gotta stand up to her.'

'We'll back you up, Miss,' said Maxine.

'Yeah, I'll hold your coat,' said Tex.

Everyone laughed at that, 'cos Tex is the last person who'd get in a fight himself. 'Specially with Mrs Barker.

Miss Summers shook her head. 'It wasn't Mrs Barker's idea,' she said. 'In any case, it's too late now. The decision's been made. I can't tell you how sorry I am.'

She didn't have to – we could see her eyes were all full up.

'Aw, Miss,' said Hemma.

Kim was patting her on the arm.

Miss Summers smiled at us and sniffed a bit. 'I told Mrs Barker I'd keep on with our practices – until the ban comes in, but she said there's not much point just for two weeks. Unless you girls really want to?'

'Of course we want to!' I blurted out. I couldn't believe it. Only two weeks of netball left and they wanted to take those away from us too.

'Yeah, come on, Miss!' said Abi. 'Don't let us down.'

Miss Summers looked at our faces. Half the team looked like they might blub any minute.

'OK. Mondays and Wednesdays as usual,' she

said, heading off into school, all sniffly and sad-looking. 'I really am sorry,' she called back to us, 'but honestly...it's out of my hands.'

Remember those words. You'll be hearing them again.

two

Standing there in the rain, with our mouths wide open, we probably didn't look much like a seriously unbeatable team. To be honest, we hardly look like a team at all. Zandra and Alicia don't really fit in – they're the sort that go mad if they get even a spot of mud on their clean netball kit. Hemma and Abi aren't like that, they're pretty tough, but pint-sized really, whereas Maxine and me are dead tall, but skinny. Kim's the only one who looks at all scary, which is a laugh, 'cos she's so shy she wouldn't say boo to a...guinea pig! She's even less scary than Tex and that's saying something.

Tex is my best buddy, but even I'd have to admit he is a bit of a wimp. It's only 'cos he's tiny – he hardly comes up to my elbow. He swears I've had all my own growth spurts and his as well. Tex isn't in the netball team, but he might as well be. He stays behind for all the practices and cheers us on at every match. He's brill. In fact, without him and his dad, things could have turned out so much worse.

The bad news was beginning to sink in for all of us. Abi was rabbiting as usual, 'It's terrible. I can't believe it! Wait till I tell my dad. Why couldn't they have waited, at least till after the league final? That's what I'd like to know.'

She kept going on, even though no one was arguing with her because she was right, 'specially about the timing. With all the rain over winter we'd missed loads of practices and so had all the other schools, so the finals had been delayed until the beginning of next term. But now, with the ban, that was gonna be too late.

Everyone had something to say, except Kim, of course. Kim hardly ever says anything, which is lucky 'cos she's Abi's best friend and never gets a word in edgeways anyway. But guess who had the last word as usual?

'It won't really bother us that much, will it?' Zandra said, turning to Alicia. 'It means we'll have more time for our dancing.'

Aaarrgh! I really wanted to tell her what I thought of her and her *dancing*. But like I said, when I get really mad it all comes out in a jumble and I end up feeling a prize twit. Right then I didn't want Zandra looking down her pointy nose at me, thanks very much. So I grabbed my bag and took off home, without saying a word. And Tex followed me.

Outside the school gates Tex's dog, Chipshop, was waiting for us. He went bananas the minute he saw us, nearly knocking Tex over in his excitement.

'How come he's always here waiting for us, whatever time we finish?' I said. 'It's like he's got his own little doggy clock.'

'If he has,' said Tex, 'it must be in his stomach.'

Tex took out a dog chew and held it up, out of Chipshop's reach. The dog started jumping in the air. His short back legs cleared the floor by a mile. Tex makes Chipshop dance like this most of the way home every day. I think it's cruel, but Tex reckons it's the only exercise the dog gets. He says Chipshop's nothing but a stomach on legs.

He says, 'Think how fat he'd be without it.'

Chipshop's real name is Rex, but everyone calls him Chipshop because that's his second home. He hangs around outside, begging for bits of fish batter, or leftover chips, which is why he's such a fat little barrel. Chipshop usually makes me laugh, whenever I see him. But he didn't that day.

We walked home, like we always do, past the bread factory, where both our dads work. I kept thinking about what Miss Summers had said – about it not being fair that some people were good at sport when other people weren't.

'It doesn't make sense,' I said to Tex. 'Why are they picking on netball? Life's not fair anyway, everybody knows that. If they want to make things fair why don't they tell the boffs to stay at home and give you and me a chance to catch up ?'

Tex laughed. 'Let's face it, that's never gonna happen.'

'And why aren't they banning the choir?' I said.

'Yeah, if we can't sing in tune, why should they let them?' said Tex. 'And what about Art Club? I can't draw to save my life.'

Where was it gonna end? 'Let's ban Zandra's hair while we're at it,' I said. 'Why should she have long blonde curls when I've got coconut matting? How can that be fair?'

Tex burst out laughing. 'I like your hair,' he said. 'It looks sorta...' I could see him trying to find the right word '...*excited*.'

I rolled my eyes and groaned. At least having Tex around, I always know there's someone dafter than me.

We were waiting to cross the road when Chipshop suddenly lost interest in his chew. He started barking fit to burst at a man putting up a poster on a wall.

'I agree with the dog,' the man said, packing up his things. 'She wouldn't get my vote either.'

We looked up at the face on the poster. The woman had a really smarmy smile, the sort that makes you think: what's she after? You know what I mean? Her eyes stared out at us from the poster, big and bulgy, like a toad's. Chipshop didn't like her one little bit.

That was the first time I ever saw Patsy Poysner.

It wasn't gonna be the last though.

Tex knew all about her. He said his dad had helped to get her on the council, though now he wished he hadn't bothered.

'He says she wants to rule the world,' Tex told me, 'and she won't stop till she does.'

'My dad doesn't trust any politicians,' I said. 'He never votes. He says, what's the point, when they're all the same.'

'They can't all be the same,' said Tex. 'And anyway, my dad says, somebody's gotta run the country.'

Well, that got me fizzing mad. 'Oh, yeah,' I yelled at him. 'With stupid rules like banning netball! That's very useful that is! The whole country'd fall apart without that one!'

Tex doesn't like arguing. He started chewing his finger ends and telling Chipshop to stop barking. But Chipshop wouldn't, so in the end we had to pick him up and carry him between us like a sack of cement, which was about what he weighed. We'd crossed the road and got right round the corner before it was safe to put him down.

Tex could see I was still mad so I think he was glad when we reached his road. 'Look, I gotta go,' he said. 'I've got my paper round to do.' He ducked off down the road with Chipshop still skipping on two legs, chasing the chew. 'See ya,' he shouted.

'Not if I see you first,' I shouted back, really

grumpy. He just waved back, dead cheerful, as if I was joking.

'I mean it,' I yelled after him, but he didn't even turn round.

After he'd gone I felt even worse. I knew Tex and all the others would miss netball, but not like I would. In fact, without netball practices, life'd be easier for them: Tex wouldn't have to rush home and race to get his paper round done. Maxine wouldn't have to persuade her next-door neighbour to mind her kid brothers twice a week. Hemma wouldn't have to drag her sister Nila with her on netball nights. Abi and Kim could go home and watch all the daytime soaps that Abi's mum tapes for her. And Alicia and Zandra – well, they had their *dancing*, didn't they!

But what about me? I'd go back to being the tall, gawky, thick one. Good at nothing and nothing to say for herself. Oh, cheers. That was really something to look forward to. Not!

three

I hate it when Tex won't argue with me. I mean, what else are best mates for? So by the time I got home I was still looking for a fight. Anyone would have done. Did I say anyone? Anyone but Gav the Taxi.

Gav was mending his clapped-out old van on our drive. Gav lives down the road but you'd never guess, 'cos he's always at my house, trying to get off with our Deedee. He's been trying since she was in Year Seven. It's never gonna happen. Gav's a real brainbox for a start. Next year he's going away to uni, so then we'll all get a bit of peace. He's supposed to be having one of those gap years and going off travelling, but it's April already and he's still here. He doesn't fool me. He thinks if he goes away our Deedee'll meet somebody else, so he hangs round ours like a love-struck doormat just waiting for her to wipe her feet on him. And he's meant to be the one with the brains!

When he spotted me, Gav waved his oily rag at me. '*Bonjour, Gelée. Ça va?*'

That's French, in case you don't know. He says it means Hiya, Jelly, how you doing? So why he can't just say that I don't know.

There were bits of engine lying all over the drive so I gave him my slit-eye look and said, 'I'd take it straight to the dump if I were you, 'cos you'll never get that lot back where it came from.'

'Maybe not,' he grinned, 'but I'll have fun finding out.'

See what I mean? No matter how hard you try you'll never get Gav to fight with you. He might have a *discussion*, if you're daft enough to let him, but he won't fight.

There's one person who always will, though.

Just then my sister, Deedee, opened the lounge window and her computer keyboard came flying out. Lucky for her, it landed in a rose bush. After it came sheets and sheets of paper like giant-size confetti.

'It's out to get me,' she yelled. 'The thing's got a life of its own. Whoever invented computers wants boiling in oil. I'm never gonna touch one again in my entire life.'

My sister Deedee's sixteen going on three and a half. She's a real drama queen. When she starts up, the rest of us usually run for cover. But not Gav. He's always been a glutton for punishment. He has to be the stupidest clever person I ever met.

He wiped his hands on his jeans and rescued the keyboard out of the rosebush. 'Hang on. I'm just coming,' he called to Deedee.

I wasn't so stupid. I'd been looking for a bit of a fight, not World War Three. I went round the side of the garage, chewed the rest of my jelly cubes – pineapple, my favourite – then practised a few nets on the back wall. Thirty out of thirty. Eas-y.

Later on, when it had all gone quiet, I guessed it was safe to go in. Deedee was sitting by the window plucking her eyebrows in a mirror while Gav sorted her computer for her. He was trying to explain what she'd done wrong, but Deedee obviously wasn't interested. 'I'm not listening,' she said. 'Me and computers are finished. History. They can whistle for their CV.'

Our Deedee's leaving school soon and she really wants a job on a fashion magazine. I told her it'd suit her, her being such a fashion victim.

'Who asked you to stick your nose in?' she shouted.

'*Enfants! Enfants!* Gav said.

'What *is* he on about?' Deedee asked me.

I don't know why she was asking me.

'*Children! Children!* Gav translated. He was waving a copy of Deedee's CV that he'd just printed off.

Suddenly she was all smiles, those sick-making

gooey ones. Oh, vomit. 'Is there anything you can't do?' she asked, flashing her eyelashes at him.

'Yeah,' I muttered. 'Talk blooming English.' Although, to be honest, he can do that as well. Sometimes Gav sounds like he's had a dictionary on toast for breakfast.

He was looking pretty pleased with himself, until Deedee plonked herself down on his knee and started plucking his eyebrows.

'Now this won't hurt,' she said.

'Ow! Ow! Deedee, stop!' Gav was yelling, but she wouldn't. Even I felt a bit sorry for him. Then Dad came downstairs and saved him.

'Deedee, put the poor lad down,' said Dad. 'Come on, Gav, I'll need you to clear your van off the drive. I'm going to work in half an hour.'

Gav escaped through the kitchen.

'You treat that lad like rubbish,' Dad told Deedee.

'Well he must like it,' she said smirking, 'or he wouldn't keep coming back for more.'

Dad named Gav 'Gav the Taxi', 'cos he waits on Deedee hand and foot and drives her anywhere she wants to go at the drop of a hat, like to her aerobics class or to meet her friends. She never invites him along, though. I told you he's wasting his time. Don't get me wrong, it's not that I don't like Gav, he's OK. I just think he should go out and get a life.

Later on, I told Mum and Dad about our netball bombshell. But they weren't really listening. Dad had to get off to work; he works shifts at the bakery. And Mum was busy cooking. 'Aw, that's tough luck, love,' she said, as if I'd just lost 5p on the way home from school.

After tea, I sat in the lounge by myself feeling really fed up. At least I could chew my jelly cubes and watch TV in peace, until Gav came in and started messing with the computer. He was doing all sorts of fancy stuff to Deedee's CV while she was upstairs, soaking herself in the bath. Soft or what?

But there's one thing about Gav, he's a good listener. I turned the TV off and gave a big sigh, hoping he'd take the hint, which he did.

'What's up, Jelly?' he asked.

I did a Deedee on him. 'I'm only eleven and my life's over,' I said. 'And there's nothing I can do about it.'

'Hmmm, sounds serious,' said Gav. 'What's happened?'

So I gave him the whole story.

When I'd finished Gav said, '*Nil desperandum.*'

'I wish you'd stop all that French!' I snapped at him.

'That was Latin,' he said. 'It means don't give up hope. Remember nothing's beyond the power of human ingenuity.'

'Can't you, *please*, just talk English for once?' I said.

'That was English!'

Well I knew that, but I meant English I could understand. He could see how fed up I was getting, though. He came and sat on the sofa by me.

'Look,' he said. 'There's bound to be a way round this.'

'No, there isn't.' I shook my head. 'Miss Summers says it's already decided. Too late. Out of her hands.'

'It's never too late,' said Gav. 'Not if you really care about something. What you need is a plan.'

'Like what?'

'Like a petition.'

'A petition?! I don't know anything about petitions,' I told him.

'You'll work it out,' said Gav. 'I've got great confidence in you, *mon ami*.'

'English!' I said through gritted teeth.

'You, *my friend*, aren't as stupid or as hopeless as you think.'

I thought, he's gotta be teasing me now, but he looked serious.

'Everyone's got their own little bit of magic inside them,' he said, 'including you, Jelly. You just don't know it yet.'

Wow! I didn't know what to say to that. But at least it'd cheered me up. He's not so bad, is he, Gav? Not quite as daft as he's cabbage-looking.

When I was lying in bed that night I thought some more about what Gav'd said. I thought, he's right, I have got my own little bit of magic and it's netball. It's being the *Shooting Star*. And that's exactly what they were trying to take away from me.

Suddenly, I thought, well, not without a fight they won't!

four

When Tex and I got into school the next day the others were looking like a wet weekend. Maxine, Hemma, Abi, Kim, Tex and me all sit together on the same table.

'Cheer up,' I said. 'We haven't lost yet.'

'My dad says we have,' Abi started up. 'He says this is what's happening today: loony people making loony decisions.' Abi's dad always has plenty to say. We think that's where she gets it from.

'Yeah, well, we don't have to give up that easy,' I said. 'We just need a plan.' I thought, how I sound like Gav.

'You tell 'em, Jelly,' Tex said.

'So, what's the plan?' asked Maxine.

'We're gonna start a petition,' I told her. 'Get everyone to sign it. Then take it to Mrs Barker.'

They were all well impressed. Kim gave me a pat on the back, which nearly made me choke. I think they were a bit surprised, 'cos I'm not usually the one with the ideas. I didn't tell them this one was Gav's really.

We got Hemma to write the petition out 'cos

her writing's better than ours. Then we took it to show Zandra and Alicia. Zandra screwed up her face. 'What's this?'

She read it out loud, like she was the teacher or something: '*I think banning netballs a rubbish idea and who ever dreamt it up must be mad.* Oh, very well put,' she said. 'Who on earth wrote this?'

Hemma went bright red. 'What's wrong with it?' she said. I went a bit red as well 'cos I was the one who'd told her what to write. Zandra shook her head and said,

'You're wasting your time.'

'I thought you two were part of this team,' said Hemma.

'In case you've forgotten, there isn't a team any more,' Zandra snapped back.

Well, that did it. I'd kept quiet until then, but now I almost shouted at her. 'And you don't care about that, do you, 'cos you've got your stupid *dancing.* But what about the rest of us? You make me sick. You don't care about anyone but yourself.'

That was quite a speech for me! But it didn't bother Zandra one little bit. 'As if you lot care about *us,*' she said. 'You've never liked me and Alicia. You think we're stuck up, don't you?'

I had to admit, she was right about most of it, 'cept we didn't mind Alicia. It was Zandra *with a zed* got on our nerves. That's what we sometimes call her 'cos she goes bananas if anyone calls her plain old *Sandra* by mistake. But we needed her now and I'd almost blown it. I made myself calm down and try again.

'Listen, it's not that we don't like you,' I said, crossing my fingers behind my back. 'We're still a team, whatever happens. No way could we win the league without you and Alicia – nor can we do this petition either.'

Then I pushed the sheet towards her and held my breath.

It worked. Zandra gave a big sigh, grabbed the petition and disappeared to the library. She did a completely new one on the computer. We all thought it was mega-impressive.

We, the undersigned, agree that banning netball in schools is completely unfair and undemocratic.

None of us could have done that. We weren't even sure what *undersigned* and *undemocratic* meant, but they sounded good. Although she got on our nerves, we had to admit, Zandra's useful sometimes.

Then we split up and went off to collect names from different groups in the class. We sent Abi and Kim to bully the football team into signing. Hemma and Maxine said they'd sort the *Pop Girls* and Tex went to talk to the *Groovy Gang*. That's what we call them anyway. They only ever talk about clothes and getting off with boys. They think Tex is cute 'cos he's small – they pat him on his head which he hates. But he said he'd put up with it, *for the sake of the petition*. I got the *Chess Nerds*. Great.

If you think the hard part was over, think again. This bit was like walking into brick walls. OK, the footballers were easy, 'cos they realised football might go the same way. But Hemma and Maxine hit trouble with the Pop Girls. There's about six of them and they spend every break in the small hall, practising dance routines. They hate going outside for PE so they said it was the best news they'd heard. Maxine tried to explain that the ban didn't mean the end of PE. But they wouldn't listen. They just kept dancing around singing: No More PE!! No More PE!!

Tex went all quiet when we asked him how he'd got on with the *Groovy Gang*. He said there were limits to what he'd go through, even for the netball team.

I didn't do any better with the *Chess Nerds*. I'd tried to explain what the petition was for but they'd kept staring at me, which made me mega nervous and I got all tongue-tied. Then, when I put the sheet in front of them and handed them a pencil, they just said, 'Do we look as if we care?'

I gave them such a mouthful then, but after that they definitely wouldn't sign. I just hoped chess was the next thing they banned. That'd serve 'em right.

By the end of the day we only had *thirty* names. Pathetic. I mean, there were the eight of us in the netball team, if you count Tex, and seven from Year 5 in the second team, plus the football team. But I wasn't gonna give up.

'We'll run off some more petitions,' I said. 'Then we can all take one home. We'll ask our mums and dads and neighbours. Anyone'll do.'

And after school I told Tex we were going home via the shops, to get even more names. 'We're gonna go into *every* shop we pass,' I told him, 'and ask everyone we meet.'

Me and my big ideas!

First we went to the off-licence. Chipshop waited outside with his paws on the window-ledge and his nose pressed against the glass making a big wet ring. He wasn't letting that chew out of his sight.

Mr Sajani was busy serving someone. While we were waiting Tex told me he'd been thinking that more people probably cared about football than netball. 'If I were you, I'd mention football as well.'

'Hmmm. I s'pose,' I said. But I wasn't convinced.

'Then you'd better write football on the petition, hadn't you?'

I was even less sure about that, but I did it. I added 'and football'. Big mistake.

Mr Sajani took one look at the petition and told us that, in his humble opinion, football was the root cause of everything that was wrong with this country. He said if he was Prime Minister the first thing he'd do was ban football. He went on for ages about football hooligans, bad language, vandalism, violence, racism...

Even after I told him the petition was really about netball, he still refused to sign. Lesson number one: never listen to Tex.

We were just about to go in the chemist and try again when Lisa, Deedee's best friend, came out and almost walked into us.

She asked what we were up to, so we told her about our petition. 'OK, let's have a look, but I'm in a hurry,' she said. I thought, good, that means she'll just sign it and go. No such luck. She told us all about her new boyfriend, Kurt, and how she was probably gonna dump him. Guess why: because he was always watching football on TV!

'I mean, he just sits there with a can in each hand,' she complained, 'swearing and yelling if his team are losing, cheering and yelling when they win. And don't even get me started on snooker. There's far too much sport on TV,' she said. 'I wish they'd ban it all.'

'It's got nothing to do with TV,' I tried to tell her.

'Or snooker,' said Tex.

'Or *football*,' I said, glaring at him.

'It says football on the petition?' said Lisa.

What could I say? Lesson number two: never, *never*, listen to Tex.

'Anyway, Jelly,' she said finally, 'I've got more important things to do than stand and listen to you pair.' As if we'd been the ones doing all the talking! 'And will you look at what that dog's done to my trousers! This is what happens when you try to do someone a favour. I wish I hadn't bothered.'

'So do I,' I said through gritted teeth. Tex had to drag me away before I said anything else I regretted.

By then I was sick of the sight of that petition. I was tempted to give it to Chipshop to eat. All the time and effort we'd put in and we still hadn't got a single new name.

Tex said. 'Why don't we go home and make up a load of names? Who's gonna know?'

'We've never won a netball match by cheating,' I said. 'And we aren't starting now.'

We walked home the rest of the way in silence.

When I got in Gav was there as usual, watching

kids' TV, his great long legs stretched out in front of him so I had to climb over them.

I said, 'Don't you think you're a bit old for kids' TV?'

'On the contrary,' he said. 'I find it very educational.'

'Yeah, right,' I said. He was watching *Rugrats*!

I started in right away about my petition and how nobody would sign it. I told him about the *Chess Nerds* and all the other wasters at school. I told him about Mr Sajani and Deedee's friend, Lisa, and Tex and his stupid idea.

'How is it nobody cares about anything except themselves?' I said.

'*C'est la vie*,' said Gav.

'Stop right there,' I snapped. I was in no mood for his French gobbledygook.

'That's life,' he quickly translated. 'But don't give up. You'll win them round in the end.'

'I haven't won anybody round yet,' I said. 'Although tomorrow I might start banging a few heads together.'

Gav grinned. 'Tempting, I'm sure, but violence is never the answer. Remember, there are different ways to crack a nut. You don't always have to use a hammer.'

I told him he'd obviously never met the *Chess Nerds*.

'Look,' said Gav, 'the secret is to win them over.

Convince them with your argument, really persuade them.'

'Are you mad?' I said. 'I'm the one who never knows what to say. At school they all think I'm thick. Nobody listens to me.'

'You never know what you're capable of,' said Gav, 'until you try.'

I couldn't even be bothered arguing with him. Just then Deedee came running downstairs. Her face was whiter than white, like she'd been dipped in a tin of paint.

'What's happened to your face?' I said.

'It's an exfoliating mask, stupid!'

'You look like you've been brought back from the dead,' I said.

Deedee glared at me, then she turned to Gav. 'I asked you to time this for ten minutes. I said, not a minute longer.'

Gav looked dead guilty. 'Sorry, I forgot. I got talking to Jelly. It's only been...' he looked at his watch, 'twenty-five minutes.'

'*Twenty-five minutes!* Deedee really went off on one then. 'If my whole face falls off you'll be to blame,' she shrieked.

I escaped upstairs then and left them to it. I slammed my bedroom door shut, threw myself on my bed and punched the wall, which really, *really* hurt.

I don't know if it was the disappointment with

the petition, or feeling so hopeless about the netball ban, or nearly breaking my fist on the wall, but I started to feel like I might cry. And I'm not the crying sort, believe me. I've nothing against it for other people. But I don't cry. Usually.

So I lay there, trying not to cry, wondering if what Gav had said was true. Perhaps I could still win the *Chess Nerds* over. Perhaps I *could* change their minds. It had to be worth a try, didn't it?

five

The next morning it didn't matter how many times I counted the names on my petition there were still only five: Mum, Dad, Mr Bowler from next door, Gav and Deedee. And Deedee only signed 'cos Gav sucked up to her. I was thinking that if the others had done as badly as me, Mrs Barker'd never take any notice of us. And then what would we do? I just had to try the *Chess Nerds* again.

I was nervous enough, but to make matters worse Tex had slept in, which is a regular thing. It's one of the reasons Mrs Barker gets so cross with both of us. Well, I have to wait for him, don't I? We raced into school long after the bell so we had no time to check out everyone else's petitions, we were straight into lessons. It was only when Miss Summers split us into groups and left us to get on with it that we got a chance to find out how the others had done. Maxine was the star. She'd gone with her mum to WeightWatchers and got everyone there to sign.

'I could've got loads more,' she said, 'but it

was full on both sides.'

No one else had even filled the first side but we'd got eighty-five names between us, without Zandra and Alicia.

'It's a flipping good start,' said Abi. 'That's what I think.'

But a *start* wasn't good enough. Even I knew you needed hundreds of names on a petition. We had a long way to go and we didn't have much time. I couldn't wait for breaktime. I was ready for a fight!

As soon as the bell went I collected the others up and said, 'Come on, *Chess Nerds* first.' We surrounded their desks; they didn't know what'd hit them.

'Now, you listen here,' I said. 'If you lot think this is nothing to do with you, you'd better think again.' I could see they hadn't the first idea what I was on about. 'The petition?!' I said, waving it in front of them.

'Don't you realise, it'll be your turn next? They'll be telling you it's not fair you being good at chess, if the rest of us aren't. Then perhaps you'll understand that netball's as important to us as chess is to you. And when you want us to sign your petition, what d'you think we're gonna say to you?'

All the others joined in with me: 'Do we look as if we care?'

The *Chess Nerds* still didn't look completely

convinced. I was starting to think banging a few heads together might be the answer after all, but I reminded myself what Gav had said about other ways to crack a nut apart from smashing it with a hammer. So I tried again.

'Listen,' I said, 'we've gotta stick together over this. It's the only way we're ever gonna beat 'em.'

'Beat who, exactly?' asked Michael Winterbottom.

'Well, we don't know who, exactly,' I said, 'not yet. But we're gonna find out.'

'And then we're gonna beat 'em,' said Tex.

'*If* we stick together,' I said, holding out the pencil. 'One for all and all for one.'

And this time they took it. Re-sult! The *Pop Girls* caved in next, then the *Groovy Gang*. Soon everyone had signed our petition and promised to take a sheet home. We had to print a copy for everyone in the class. It was magic.

'Two-four-six-eight, who do we appreciate? *Jelly!* said Tex, doing a little victory dance.

'Yeah, you're a star,' Maxine said, patting me on the back.

Then a voice behind me said, 'Yes, well done, Jelly.' It was Zandra. I could hardly believe my ears. Ever since I'd told her we couldn't win the league without her she'd been quite pally. Of course, the next minute she was showing off about how she and Alicia had both got their petitions full already. I kept mine folded in my pocket. It looked a bit pathetic compared with theirs.

We hadn't told Miss Summers what we were up to. It hadn't been easy keeping it a secret but we wanted to get the petitions full first. I think she knew we were up to something, though, 'cos I noticed her watching me a few times in class, and after school in netball practice. It was the first practice we'd had since she told us about the ban. I may be hopeless at sums but even I can count to three and that's all the netball practices we'd got left, including this one, unless our petition worked. Thinking about that just made me feel sick inside.

I guess everyone was feeling the same because when we started playing we were *rubbish*. The Year 5 second team were really giving us the run-around. Hemma and Alicia kept fluffing their passes. Zandra was hogging the ball even worse than usual. Kim and Abi missed the action at least once 'cos they were gossiping. And Tex wasn't cheering us on like he usually did. Even Miss Summers didn't look as if her heart was in it. Oh, no, I thought, not you as well, Miss.

Seeing everybody else had given up just made me twice as determined. I was everywhere; all over the court, wherever I was allowed, and once or twice where I wasn't. I was cheering everyone else on, telling them, *Great pass! Brill shot!* even when it wasn't. I felt like next door's puppy, all legs and no brain, rushing about licking everyone.

At last it began to work. The others woke up and started to try a bit harder. Every time Zandra got the ball I yelled, *Go Zandra, go!* 'cos I know how much that helps me. And she did seem to move faster, find the spaces better, and get rid of the ball quicker. She even smiled at me a couple of times, like I was a friend, which felt sort of funny, but...OK.

And finally we were like Miss Summers sometimes says: on song. When we're really working as a team we sort of know where each other is, without having to look, and the passes are smooth as butter. It's like we've got magic in our hands and our feet. And I love it.

Tex woke up at last. 'Fly, Jelly, fly!' he yelled every time I went for a goal. 'Here comes the *Shooting Star*!' And I jumped higher than I'd ever jumped before, right over the basket and I watched the ball drop to the ground underneath me. Sometimes I imagine I could float through the ring after it, like I'm made of rubber, and land in this dead flashy handstand and everyone'd cheer and clap and shout, 'Way to go, Jelly!'

Yeah, I know – in my dreams.

At the end of the practice Miss Summers told us

we were *magnificent*! She said it was a crying shame we wouldn't get a crack at the final. Then she broke off and sniffed a couple of times while we all looked down at our feet.

'And, Jelly...' she said, turning to me and giving me this big grin. 'I don't know what your mum's feeding you, but I think we'd better put the rest of the team on it.' Everyone laughed and I started to go red and wish she'd stop right there, but she didn't. 'In fact, if you were to keep this up – I mean... if we'd been able to carry on with the league – we'd have to seriously think about letting you have a turn as captain. Don't you think, Zandra?'

Wow! That was the last thing I ever expected to hear. I was so chuffed. I knew I'd played well though, even if that does make me sound big-headed. But it hadn't done me any favours with Zandra. She's always been the captain; she was glaring at me like I'd stabbed her in the back.

Tex cheered me up on the way home though, doing this wicked impression of her.

'My name's Zandra,' he whined, '*with a zed.*'

Anyway Zandra was the least of my worries.

'D'you think we're gonna get enough names to persuade Mrs Barker?' I asked Tex.

'Honestly or not honestly?' he said, dead serious for a minute.

I thought, oh no, even Tex thinks we're wasting

our time. But he broke out into this great big grin. 'No contest,' he said. 'It's in the bag. Give me some skin, *Shooting Star*.' And we skinned palms.

I could've hugged him then. 'Course I didn't. You don't do that kinda thing with buddies. But I did give him a couple of my jelly cubes. Not the pineapple ones, though. I'm not that daft.

six

At breaktime on Thursday morning we were all standing in a huddle in Mrs Barker's office while Zandra gave her the petition. There were sheets and sheets of it. I still couldn't believe we'd got nine hundred and thirty-two names! Miss Summers was really proud of us. She'd said Mrs Barker was bound to be impressed too. And she did look it.

It had been my idea that Zandra should hand the petition to Mrs Barker. She was the captain, after all. And everybody knows Zandra's Mrs Barker's favourite. You can tell by the way Mrs Barker talks to her as if the rest of us aren't even there.

'Oh well done, dear. You've clearly gone to a lot of trouble.'

'Everyone's been very busy,' Miss Summers tried to tell her. 'Jelly especially.'

But Mrs Barker just ignored her. 'I like to see a bit of initiative, Zandra. And I do have some sympathy with your point of view, but I'm afraid it isn't a school matter. This is a council decision.'

Suddenly she was handing the sheets back. She hadn't even read any of the names. 'I'm sorry,' she said, 'but...it's out of my hands.'

I told you you'd hear those words again! I just went up like a rocket. 'So, just whose hands is it in then, I'd like to know?'

Mrs Barker gave me a long hard look, but then she carried on talking to Zandra. 'The Education Committee have left us no choice by withdrawing our insurance. So I'm afraid that's an end to the subject.'

She stared at me, sort of daring me to say anything else. So I did.

'But why does that matter?' I asked.

Mrs Barker looked over her glasses at me. 'Because, young lady, if one of you has an accident while playing netball, you might sue the school. And we can't afford that if we don't have insurance.'

'We'll make sure we don't fall over,' said Maxine.

'And if we do we'll promise not to sue,' said Hemma.

'I'm afraid that would be your parents' decision,' said Mrs Barker.

'We'll make them promise not to sue,' said Maxine.

Mrs Barker shook her head and turned back to her computer, which meant that she wanted us to go, but I was feeling like Chipshop with a chew.

I just couldn't let go.

'But what about our petition?' I said. 'What about all the names we've collected?'

Mrs Barker just shrugged as if that wasn't her problem. Miss Summers was sorry for us, though. 'Couldn't they at least send their petition to the council?' she asked.

Mrs Barker sighed. 'It's almost certainly too late to do any good.'

'But it can't do any harm,' Miss Summers argued.

'I suppose not,' Mrs Barker said. 'Yes, yes, all right.' You could see she just wanted to get rid of us.

But Miss Summers kept on. 'So who should they send it to?' Mrs Barker didn't even look up.

'Mrs Poysner is the chairperson. But she's a very busy lady, so don't expect a reply.'

'That's that woman on the poster,' Tex whispered to me. 'D'you remember?' I thought, not her with the horrible eyes.

'You'll find the address of the Town Hall on the Internet,' Mrs Barker told Zandra. 'It'll be a useful little exercise for you.'

As we were leaving she said to Miss Summers, 'I suppose it can't hurt for the council to see that our children are interested in local issues. You know what they say, no publicity's bad publicity.'

You'll hear *those* words again, as well.

We headed back to the classroom. I wasn't feeling very hopeful. I was glad when Zandra and Alicia went off to the library, 'cos Zandra had *I told you so* written all over her face and I was sick of seeing it.

'Miss Summers did say it can't do any harm,' Hemma said, trying to look on the bright side.

'Yeah, but Mrs Barker said it's probably too late,' said Maxine.

'Oh, cheer me up, why don't you?' I said.

Miss Summers came and sat with us at our table. 'Don't be fed up,' she said. 'Sometimes you just have to accept you've done the best you can and that's all you can do.'

'But we can't stop now, Miss. We've gotta keep trying,' I said. I told her what Gav had said. 'There's lotsa ways to crack a nut, you know, apart from using a hammer.'

Miss Summers burst out laughing and squeezed my arm. I don't know why, but at least I seemed to have cheered *her* up.

At the end of the morning she read us a *Just William* story. He's one of her favourites. He's such an idiot it always make her giggle when she reads about him and then that makes us laugh as well. But it gave me an idea. William might be an idiot but he always manages to make things happen. He wouldn't be wasting time sending petitions to committees at the Town Hall. He'd go straight to the top. And I told the others that's what we should do.

'Yeah,' said Tex. 'Way to go, Jelly. We'll take it to the Prime Minister. I seen 'em handing in petitions to Downing Street on the telly.'

'I said, straight to the top, you twit, not over the top.'

I meant this woman – Patsy whatever-her-name-is. If we could get to her, face to face, we could explain to her why she'd got it all wrong and persuade her to forget the ban.

We found Zandra and Alicia in the library, still on the computer.

'What do you lot want?' Zandra asked. So friendly – not!

I told her my idea. Surprise, surprise, she wasn't very pleased.

'You mean to say we've spent an hour on the Internet for nothing?'

I don't know who she thought she was kidding – we'd just caught them looking at a site where they could buy ballet shoes on line.

'Anyway,' Zandra snapped at me, 'how are we going to find out where *she* lives? Because I can tell you for nothing, she doesn't live in the Town Hall.'

'I know that, ' I said. 'I'm not stupid.'

'You could have fooled me,' said Zandra.

'I don't see you coming up with a better idea,'

I told her.

'Look, I—' Tex started, but Zandra cut him off.

'This is nothing to do with you,' she snapped. 'This is netball business. You can keep right out of it.'

'Please yourself,' Tex shrugged. 'I was only gonna say I know where she lives, 'cos I've been to her house with my dad to collect leaflets.'

'Why didn't you tell us that before?' I almost shouted.

'Nobody asked me,' he said, grinning.

'Right,' I said, giving him a friendly punch, 'we can all go tomorrow after school.'

'Hang on,' he said. 'We went in my dad's car. She lives right in the middle of town.'

'Don't worry about that,' I said. 'I know someone who'll take us.'

'Alicia and I can't possibly go tomorrow,' said Zandra, all stuck up again. 'It's our—'

'...*dancing class*,' Maxine and Hemma piped up together.

'This is important you know,' I told Zandra.

'And our dancing class isn't?'

'I'm not saying that. It's just that this is more ...urgent.'

'Surely, we don't all need to go,' she said.

'But we do. That's the whole point,' I told her. 'We have to turn up as a team. Show we're together on this one.'

I wasn't going to give in, but neither was Zandra. All the others were standing behind me, watching to see who was gonna win. It was like a showdown in a cowboy film.

Suddenly Alicia said, 'Couldn't we miss dancing, Zandra, just this once?'

Zandra looked at her like she was the biggest traitor in town. In the end she gave one of her sighs and said, 'I'll have to think about it.'

'Good,' I said. 'And while you're at it you can decide whether you're really in this team. Or not.'

'You tell her, Jelly,' Tex whispered.

Zandra gave him a real icy look. 'I'm still captain, in case you've all forgotten,' she reminded us.

I said, 'Then you'll be there, won't you? Any real captain would be.'

The others just stared, like they couldn't believe their ears. 'Cos no one ever gets the last word with Zandra. It was a toss up who was most surprised: Zandra or me.

seven

Just as I was leaving school my mum collared me in the cloakroom. That's the worst thing about having your mum working at your school.

'I want you to go shopping,' she said. 'I've done you a list and Gav says he'll take you in his van.'

No way! Shopping with Gav! What if anyone saw me? I'd never live it down.

We stood there having this big battle. Guess who won?

On the way home I was moaning to Tex, but he didn't understand. 'What's the big problem?'

'Gav's the big problem,' I snapped. 'Him and his wrinkly old van. He's Deedee's stupid boyfriend, not mine. At least he'd like to be.'

'So, why doesn't your mum ask her to go?' asked Tex.

' 'Cos *she'd* hit the roof!' I yelled. 'Mum's scared of Deedee and her rotten temper, that's why.'

Tex changed the subject, like he always does if I get a bit rattled. 'So how are we getting to Patsy Poysner's house tomorrow?'

'I'm gonna ask Gav, aren't I?' I sort of mumbled.

'Ohhh, would that be the same Gav who's too much of a geek to be seen dead shopping with?' he asked.

'You can shut up,' I told him. 'This is different.'

'Oh, yeah, I can see that,' Tex said, smirking. 'Anyway, now you'll be able to ask him for that lift while you're buying your frozen peas,' he said, ducking off down his road before I could get him. Chipshop raced after him, his tail wagging nineteen to the dozen. Tex looked so pleased with himself, if he'd had a tail it would've been wagging as well.

When I got home Gav said we'd got to get straight off to the supermarket because he'd promised to take Deedee into town later. She was going on a girls' night out. I nearly asked him why she didn't just book herself a taxi, then I realised she had.

At the supermarket, as we were going round, I told Gav all about Mrs Barker and the petition and about how she'd said we could send it to the Town Hall. But I told him we were gonna do better than that.

'We're going straight to the top,' I said, dead proud of myself. 'To this Patsy what's-her-name. We're gonna tell her it was a crazy idea in the first place and she's gotta change her mind. Now, or else!'

Gav said. 'Very elegantly put.'

'Oh, don't start with that,' I said. 'I don't care as long as she changes her mind. And she will, when she hears what we've got to say.'

'Look, Jelly,' he said, going all serious on me, 'it may not be as simple as that.' I turned and gave him a hard stare, like Mrs Barker gives me. 'I'm just warning you,' he said, 'it's beginning to sound like a *fait accompli.*'

'English!' I nearly screamed.

'It means it's already decided,' he explained. 'A done-deal.'

'But *you* were the one who told me it's never too late,' I yelled at him. '*You* said all we needed was a plan and our own little bit of magic. Now you're trying to tell me I might as well give up? Well, I won't. I'll show *you*. I'll show all of you.'

Suddenly Gav was grinning his head off. He started clapping.

'Bravo, Jelly. You're right,' he said. 'Don't give up the fight. You could win yet.' And he raised his fist. '*Vive la Revolution!* which means, he explained, 'Long Live the Revolution! Even you have to agree, that sounds better in French. It's got more of a ring to it. Like I keep telling you: you have to use the best words you can. Express yourself elegantly.'

'Honestly, you do talk a load of twaddle,' I said. '*Express yourself elegantly!* You should get out more.'

But Gav got serious again. 'All I'm saying is: yes,

it's important to have a bit of passion, but you've still got to get your message across. Like you did with the Chess Nerds, eventually?' he reminded me.

'Hmmm, I s'pose,' I grunted.

Then Gav started juggling with tins of baked beans and while he was in such a good mood I made sure I asked for a lift to Patsy Poysner's.

'Yeah, why not,' he grinned, grabbing a floor mop I'd just taken off the shelf and waving it in the air. 'Always happy to support the revolution.'

But Gav's mood changed as soon as he saw the queues at the checkout. 'Now we're going to get caught in the teatime traffic,' he moaned. 'Deedee's going to be hopping mad.'

When we finally came out of the supermarket, loaded down with bags of shopping, you'll never believe who we nearly ran into. Only Patsy Poysner herself! I recognised the smarmy smile straight off.

'That's the woman we're taking the petition to,' I told Gav.

'Mmmm, best of luck,' he said. 'Come on.'

But I wanted a closer look. People were queuing up to shake her hand as if she was the queen or something. She was smiling and patting their kids on their heads, asking them if they were going to vote for her in the elections.

Suddenly I felt so mad I just dumped my bags

of shopping at Gav's feet and said, 'I'm gonna go and tell the old toad now.' But Gav grabbed hold of me.

'There's no time now,' he said. 'Anyway it's not a good idea.'

'Why not?' I said.

'Have you got the petition with you?' he asked.

'Does it look like I have?'

'And have you worked out exactly what you want to say to her?'

'Not exactly,' I said.

'OK,' said Gav. 'Try it out on me first.'

He stood there surrounded by all the shopping bags in the middle of the car park. We were causing a real hold-up, but Gav didn't seem to care.

He was right, I didn't know what I wanted to say, not if I stopped to think about it first.

'I rest my case,' said Gav. 'I've been trying to tell you – you're only going to get one chance at this. So make sure you don't waste it by talking rubbish, or losing your temper! Now pick those bags up,' he went on, 'and let's go.'

I'd never seen this bossy side of Gav before. I thought, he should try it on Deedee.

We set off home in silence, which suited me fine. I was thinking of all the things I might have said, if Gav had let me. OK, so they wouldn't have been *elegant* but at least I'd have got them off my chest.

Gav wasn't very happy either. By now we were crawling along in the teatime traffic. His clapped out old van started making coughing noises, like it had smoked far too many cigarettes.

'Sounds like it's about to croak,' I said.

'Don't you worry about *Evie*. She's fine,' Gav said, patting the dashboard. He calls his van Evie because of his number plate, EV11 0NZ. 'You just have to treat her with a bit of respect.'

OK, OK, I thought. I knew he was worried he was gonna get an earful from our Deedee. But when we got home Mum said she'd caught the bus instead. She'd left Gav a message, stuck to the computer screen: *People shouldn't make promises they have no intention of keeping.*

'Don't worry, love,' Mum said. 'You know Deedee, she'll get over it. You sit down. I'll make us a cuppa.' And while Mum made his tea, I decided it was my turn to hand out some advice.

'You know you're going about it all wrong with our Deedee,' I said 'Your trouble is: you try too hard, you're far too keen, and – worst of all – you're always there! That's never gonna work with my sister. You've gotta stand up to her and stop acting like a doormat. Then she might appreciate you more.'

After I'd finished Gav looked even flatter than before, like I'd rolled him out with a rolling pin. Love's a terrible thing. I hope I never have to go through it. I felt sorry for Gav but all I could think was now I'd upset him, just when I was relying on him for a lift. I thought, me and my big mouth.

Gav was sitting there in silence, letting his tea go cold. In the end I just had to ask him, 'You will still take us tomorrow, won't you, Gav?'

He managed this pathetic little smile. 'Oh, yeah,' he said. 'Don't worry, Jelly. You can always rely on Gav the Taxi.'

I went bright red. I hadn't even realised he knew we called him that.

eight

On Friday at half past three we were all outside the school gates waiting for Gav to arrive. Zandra had decided she could miss her dancing lesson, *just this once*. We hadn't told Mrs Barker or Miss Summers about our plan, in case they tried to put us off. But Miss Summers was outside on bus duty and as we were driving off Abi couldn't resist waving the petition out of the window, and shouting, 'Wish us luck, Miss.'

Like I said, we don't call her gabby for nothing.

Everyone giggled when Gav said, 'Welcome, *compadres*,' and other silly stuff and got us singing, 'We're all going on a Re-vo-looo-tion.' I realised I must be getting used to him, 'cos I'd almost forgotten how weird he was.

Evie was rattling and banging again. No one else seemed to notice, but I heard Zandra whisper to Alicia, 'Bit of a rust bucket, isn't it?'

That really got up my nose. 'For your information,' I told her, 'this van may be old but she's full of character.' I soon wished I hadn't because almost straight away Evie gave up the ghost and stopped dead at the side of the road.

'Mmmm, bags of character,' Zandra sneered. 'Pity she doesn't actually go.'

Luckily we'd nearly reached Patsy Poysner's house.

'It's only round the corner,' Gav said. 'You lot carry on.'

'But aren't you coming?' I asked him.

'Don't worry, I'll fix her in no time and follow you. This is your battle, Jelly, I'm just the transport. But try to remember...express yourself elegantly.'

Did I say I'd forgotten what a weirdo he was?! Everyone looked at me, wondering what he meant. I just rolled my eyes.

'Don't ask,' I said.

We all got out and wandered down the street till we found the right house. It was really big, with lots of steps up to the front door. Tex had told us it was pretty flash, but even so, looking up at that shiny doorknocker made us all go quiet.

'So who's gonna do it?' said Maxine.

Everybody was looking at me. 'I think Zandra should,' I said.

'It was your stupid idea, not mine,' Zandra snapped.

'Oh, let's get on with it,' said Tex and he sprinted up the steps. I thought what a star he was, and how I wouldn't ever call him a wimp again until he ran back down and hid behind the rest of us!

When the door opened we were all a bit surprised. We didn't expect Patsy Poysner to open it herself. I was expecting a maid or a butler or someone. She seemed really annoyed that we'd disturbed her. I couldn't work out why she kept peering down the street. I don't know who she thought we'd brought with us. Then she put on her smarmy smile, just like on the poster. It was a good job we hadn't brought Chipshop with us. He'd have gone bananas.

'Yes?' she said. 'Can I help you?' Her voice was dead snooty. I gave Zandra a nudge and stuck the envelope in her hand.

'Hello, Mrs Poysner,' Zandra said. 'We've come from St Stephen's School. We've brought a petition.'

'A petition, how very interesting,' Mrs Poysner said. She wasn't interested enough to ask what it was about, though.

I hissed at Zandra, 'Tell her what it says.'

'It's about the sports ban,' said Zandra. 'We were wondering—'

'What I'd like to know,' Mrs Poysner cut her off, 'is whose idea was it? Did some reporter put you up to this?'

'No, it was our idea,' said Zandra.

'Now, come on,' she said, as if we were teasing her. 'You didn't get all the way here on your own, I'm sure.'

'Gav the Taxi brought us,' I said.

She looked at me like I'd just said aliens had dropped us off.

'What I can't understand is why you've come *here*. Does this look like the Town Hall?' No one spoke but we all shook our heads. 'No, it doesn't, does it? You really can't come bothering me at home. There are rules, you know, procedures for this kind of thing.'

I caught Zandra's eye, she'd gone really pink in the face and it had *I-told-you-so* written all over it. But we'd come all this way and I wasn't going home till we'd said our piece.

'We just want to talk to you about this stupid netball ban,' I said. OK, I admit it came out a bit louder than I meant it to.

She narrowed her eyes and came down a couple of steps for a closer look at me.

'Well,' she said, smiling her smarmy smile again, 'there's nothing I'd like better than to sit and discuss this with you all. It's a matter very close to my heart. It was my idea in the first place in fact. But I'm far too busy so I suggest you ring the Town Hall. My secretary will send you the minutes of the meeting where it was decided. Thank you and goodbye.'

She was already closing the door. I couldn't bear it.

'*But it's not fair,*' I suddenly found myself wailing.

She turned back and stared at me. 'Fair?!' she almost laughed. 'That's exactly my point. This will help to make schools fairer, less competitive. You people are the lucky ones. You obviously like all that rushing around with hockey sticks...'

'*Netball,*' everyone said, but she wasn't listening.

'But I'm concerned about those other less fortunate children who aren't good at sports.'

'Yeah, but they've got other things that we haven't,' said Abi. 'Chess and choir.'

'And violins and things,' said Tex.

'And *dancing,*' said Maxine, having another little dig at Zandra.

'I haven't got time for this nonsense,' Mrs Poysner snapped. 'There's nothing I can do now, even if I wanted to. It's already gone through committee. By this time next week it will have been approved. So, you see, I'm afraid...*it's completely out of my hands.*'

Oh, well, that was it. When I heard those words I grabbed the envelope off Zandra and ran up the steps.

'Not any more,' I said, stuffing the petition into her hands. 'Here. Now it isn't. See what you think about that!'

She stepped back. 'You...rude child!' she

gasped. She wasn't exactly breathing fire yet, but when she looked down and saw the envelope, she suddenly looked as if she might.

'I suppose this your idea of a joke?' she exploded. She threw the petition back at us and went inside, slamming the door.

'What was that about?' said Hemma, after we'd all stood there for a few seconds in stunned silence.

'Search me,' said Abi.

None of us knew what was going on, until Zandra picked up the envelope and asked, 'Which cretin wrote this?! Oh, let me guess.'

I went bright red. OK, I knew it wasn't my best handwriting, but I couldn't understand why that should have made her blow her stack.

Zandra waved the envelope under my nose, yelling, 'That's not how you spell *Poysner*, you lame-brain. Or Patsy.' She held the envelope up for everyone to see.

'*PASTY POISONER*,' she read. 'What a botch-up.'

'It wasn't my fault!' I yelled. 'I told Tex to get the spelling off Miss Summers.'

We all turned to Tex. 'She was busy,' he shrugged, 'so I asked one of the *Chess Nerds*. They said that's how you spelled it.'

Gav turned up just then, having fixed his van. He thought it was a great joke, which started everyone else laughing. Even Zandra. But I knew she was really laughing at me for getting it wrong again. I felt like a prize twit. Patsy Poysner was already against us, now she probably hated us too. Tex tried cheering me up with one of his silly jokes, but I said, 'Just zip it.'

'What? What did I do?' he said. Sometimes he doesn't have a clue.

I think everyone must have caught my bad mood because soon we were all sitting in Gav's van like a load of flat tyres.

'Come on. You did your best,' Gav told us. '*Nil desperandum.*'

I saw the smug look on his face when I told the others that meant don't give up.

'It's easy for you to say,' I told him. 'But time's running out. By next week she said it'll really be too late.'

'Which means you've got a whole week left,' said Gav. 'You'll come up with another plan.' He sounded so confident, for a minute everyone seemed to believe him.

'OK, who wants dropping off where?' Gav asked, like a regular taxi.

I said, 'You don't seem very bothered that Deedee's probably waiting at home, watching the clock.'

'She'll have to wait, won't she?' he said, smiling. 'I can't always be there, just in case she wants me.

I don't want to look too keen, do I?'

I was dead surprised. I thought, perhaps there is hope for him yet.

When I got home the first thing I did was take the petition out and tear the envelope up into a hundred tiny pieces and flush them down the loo. All evening I tried not to think about Patsy Poysner. But when I got into bed odd bits kept popping into my head. Every time I thought about getting her name wrong I went hot all over with embarrassment. Even worse, I knew Zandra was never gonna let me live it down. Not in a million years.

nine

I'd tried my hardest that weekend to come up with a plan, but by Monday all I'd managed was to give myself a headache. Mum said I looked like I was coming down with something and perhaps I should stay at home, but as things turned out it was lucky I went in because Tex had a plan. He was turning into a real life-saver. He'd gone home and told his dad all about *Pasty the Poisoner* – that's what we were calling her by then. His dad said we shouldn't waste our time on *her*. We should go and see Stan Edgar, a mate of his who was on the council.

'He only lives round the corner from us,' Tex said. 'My dad says we might get a bit more sympathy from him.'

'OK. But it's not sympathy we want,' I said. 'It's action.'

Well, we got that all right. Just before breaktime the whole netball team was sent for – to go to straight to Mrs Barker's office!

'Now we're for it,' said Maxine.

We just knew *Pasty the Poisoner* must have complained and we were in for big trouble. Zandra was fizzing mad and blamed it all on me.

'Now look what you've got us into,' she snapped. 'I'm already in trouble with my mum and dad for going in the first place, and with my dance teacher for missing my lesson. I'm sick of the whole business. No way am I taking the blame for any more of your crazy ideas, Jelly Jackson. I've a good mind not to come.'

But she didn't have a choice, any more than we did. We stood outside the office like we were on our way to jail. And when Mrs Barker buzzed for us to come in, the others pushed me in first. It wasn't *all* my fault.

But we started to relax when we saw Mrs Barker was smiling. 'I have a rather nice surprise for you all,' she said.

There were two young men in her office. They were smiling as well.

'This is Mr Cox from the local newspaper,' Mrs Barker said. 'He's heard about your petition. He'd like to write a piece about it. And Mr Harvey is going to take your photograph. Isn't that exciting?'

'You can call us Leo, and this is Ben,' said the reporter, who was dead dishy, like Brad Pitt. 'Yep, we're going to make you all famous.'

'Now, Zandra, explain to Mr Cox how it all started.'

The reporter got out his notepad. 'OK, Sandra, fire away.'

'It's not Sandra,' she said firmly. 'It's Zandra – *with a zed*.'

We all had to bite our lips to stop ourselves from laughing.

Zandra wasn't looking sick of the whole business now. She was making out it had all been her idea. She kept smiling at Leo and playing with her hair, like our Deedee when she's trying to get round Gav. Oh, vomit. But the worst of it was: she left out all the important bits and told him daft stuff, like how she'd once auditioned for *Les Miserables*.

'Of course I love netball,' she told him, 'but if I had to choose it would have to be my dancing career.'

I couldn't believe my ears! I kept whispering, trying to remind her that this was about netball, not dancing, but she just ignored me.

Leo looked completely bored. 'What about the rest of you?' he asked. 'What do you think about this ban?'

Abi was about to start up, but that would've been nearly as bad as Zandra, so I jumped in first. 'We think it's plain stupid,' I said. 'You'd have to be completely loony to have dreamt it up. It's supposed to be about making things fair, but this has to be the most unfair thing I've ever heard of.'

Leo was writing dead fast. 'Go on,' he said, 'this is very interesting. Just what I wanted.'

So I carried on: 'Next thing, they'll be chopping me and Maxine off at the knees, 'cos we're bigger than the rest. And banning the boffs from coming to school. But what good would that do? They can't help being clever, no more than I can help being a beanpole, or Zandra can help having curly hair. Or we can help being good at netball. It's crazy.'

I was really getting into it, and Leo was writing down everything I said, until Mrs Barker butted in.

'Thank you, Angelina,' she said, pushing me right to the back. 'I think that's quite enough for now.'

Leo looked dead pleased with me, even if Mrs Barker didn't. He said it was a real scoop and he asked for my name. He said if he hurried back he might be in time to make tonight's edition. I thought, I'm gonna be in the paper! Wow! Wait till my mum and dad find out.

Then we all had to go into the hall while Ben took a photo. They made me stand in the middle holding a netball really high while Hemma and Abi tried to get it off me, which was just plain stupid because they're the smallest. Then they made the others bob down round the back so you could hardly see them. I couldn't see the point of that. Mrs Barker seemed a bit cross with Leo before he left.

But he said, 'You know what they say, Mrs Barker, no publicity's bad publicity.'

Mrs Barker didn't look as if she agreed, which was a surprise to me 'cos I'd heard her say the same thing herself only the other day. When she saw us all listening she said, 'Back to the classroom, all of you. I'm sure you've got lots of work to catch up on.'

Then she gave me a very odd look. You can tell I'm definitely not one of her favourites.

When we told Tex all about the reporter, he was grinning from ear to ear. I was surprised he was *so* pleased.

Until Hemma said, 'Who d'you think told the papers anyway?'

And Tex burst out, 'It was my dad! He's got a mate works on the paper.'

Honestly, I couldn't believe it. Tex's dad seems to have mates everywhere. But the biggest surprise was that Tex hadn't told us. He's never kept a secret from me for five minutes before. He was so excited he couldn't sit still for a second. Miss Summers had to get quite cross with him.

'Tex! Bottom!'

'Miss?'

'Sit on it!'

After school we had a short netball practice. Miss

Summers had a dentist's appointment and had to leave early.

'But I'll make it up to you on Wednesday,' she said. 'We'll make it really special since that'll be...' She trailed off, but we all knew what she'd been going to say. After that I don't think anybody's heart was in it. Even mine. Anyway we were all dying to get home to see if there was anything in the newspaper.

'I bet we'll be on the front page,' Abi said.

'It's not exactly headline news, is it?' Zandra sneered.

'It might be. You never know,' said Hemma.

'In your dreams,' said Zandra.

She's such a know-it-all sometimes.

I suddenly thought, with us finishing early, why not go and see this Stan Edgar today.

'Who's coming with us?' I asked.

Maxine couldn't because she had her kid brothers to collect from next door. 'I'm really sorry,' she said.

Of course, Zandra wasn't sorry. 'We can't possibly go today,' she snapped. 'My mum'll be picking Alicia and me up any minute.'

I didn't say anything this time because after her performance in the morning I was quite glad she couldn't come. But it didn't stop *her* having a go at *me*.

'Oh, and Jelly,' she said, with that sick-making

smile of hers, 'try not to shoot your mouth off this time. And you will make sure you've spelled his name right on the envelope, won't you?'

Oooh, I could've just....but I didn't. Anyway, I'd already got a new envelope off Miss Summers and I wasn't taking any chances. I'd left it blank. See, I'm not so stupid!

ten

So the five of us that were left: Abi, Kim, Tex, Hemma and me, set off together. *And* Chipshop, which I just knew wasn't gonna be a good idea. Plus Hemma's sister, Nila, who has to go everywhere with us.

'It'd drive me mad if I had to trail a kid sister with me wherever I go,' I told Tex. 'How come Hemma never seems to mind?'

'Hemma's Hemma,' said Tex.

'What kind of answer's that?'

'Well, she's not like you, is she?'

'Meaning?'

'She's dead laid back. She doesn't have a temper for a start.'

'Temper?! I haven't got a temper,' I snapped. 'You should live with our Deedee. She's the one with the temper. I can't believe you just said that!'

Tex grinned and shrugged. Like I said, he never argues with me.

As we got closer, I asked, 'What's he like, this Stan Edgar?'

'I dunno, but don't worry,' said Tex. 'My dad

says his heart's in the right place.'

I said I hoped it was for his sake – it wouldn't do him much good behind his ear, would it?

OK, bad joke, I know and I suppose I had been a *bit* bad-tempered. But it was all 'cos I was starting to feel nervous about turning up at this man's door, 'specially after how things had gone with *Pasty the Poisoner*. I was really hoping this visit would go better though. I might not be able to manage Gav's elegant blahdy-blah but I was sure – just this once – I could keep my mouth under control. I had to, it was a matter of life and death.

Stan Edgar's wife was dead nice. When we told her why we'd come she invited us straight in and made a real fuss of Chipshop. She gave us a biscuit each, and one for the dog. They were chocolate Hobnobs! Tex was dead chuffed.

'Good start,' he whispered to me. Tex is like Chipshop – always happiest when he's got a biscuit in his mouth.

Mrs Edgar told us her husband was down the garden but we could go and find him. 'He'll be busy in his vegetable patch,' she said, smiling.

'Don't worry,' Tex told her, 'Chipshop'll sniff him out.'

I can't say Mr Edgar looked too pleased to be sniffed out. He was in the middle of planting potatoes in a big trench and he didn't seem to want to stop and talk to us. He kept on digging and telling us to watch where we were stepping and to *keep that dog out of trouble*!

There was a quite a big pile of manure nearby and Abi and Kim were holding their noses and giggling. Mr Edgar said, 'If you don't like the smell, don't stand so blooming close.' He had a point, the daft pair were nearly standing in it.

I nudged Tex to get him started. He told Mr Edgar we'd come about the netball ban.

'Not just netball,' Mr Edgar grumbled. 'All competitive sports. Daftest idea I ever heard.'

That was a good start. At least he agreed with us.

Tex told him, 'We tried to talk to *Pasty the...*' Hemma nudged him, just in time, 'Mrs Poysner.'

'Wasting your time there, lad,' Mr Edgar said. 'I bet she sent you off with a flea in your ear.'

Tex grinned. 'Yeah, but my dad said you might be able to help.'

'Humph,' Stan Edgar grunted. 'He did, did he?' Then he started grumbling, about how he might have been able to help, once upon a time, but now things were pushed through the council without folks like him getting a chance to have their say. He told us he was glad to be retiring. He felt sorry for kids like us – what kind of a world were we growing up in? And loads more like it. I suppose it was sympathy, but it was about as much use to us as a chocolate teapot. Like I said, we needed action.

All the time he was talking Stan Edgar was telling us to move out of his way, pass him his tools, or keep that wretched animal off his leeks. We weren't getting anywhere. I tried to catch Tex's eye, to get him to have one last try, but he was far too busy licking the chocolate off his second biscuit. I don't know how he managed to get two!

'So what *can* we do, Mr Edgar?' I finally had to ask.

'Nowt. Probably too late by now.' He shook his head. 'The Scrutiny Committee meets on Thursday but it's not even on our agenda – she made sure of that. I'm sorry, kids, it's not my department. I'm afraid it's...' I thought, I know what's coming next, 'out of my hands.'

I really lost it then – I mean, big time. I flung my bag down and I didn't care when it landed on top of his precious potatoes.

'If I hear one more person say *it's out of their hands* I'm gonna do something dangerous,' I shouted. '*It's gotta be in somebody's hands!*'

'There's no need to shout, young lady,' Mr Edgar said.

But by then I couldn't stop myself. No, I won't shout, I thought, I'll yell instead. So I did.

'You're just as bad as her,' I told him. 'You say you care about kids, but you don't.

'You just want to retire and plant rotten potatoes that you can buy for 50p a bag at the corner shop! My dad's right, you politicians, you're all the same – you only care about yourselves. I'm never going to vote, ever, in my whole life, 'cos it's just a whopping waste of time.'

Well, that made Stan Edgar stop digging. He stared at me with his mouth wide open.

'Now, you listen to me, young lady—' he shouted back.

But all the noise had got Chipshop really excited. He suddenly started barking and dived into the trench, digging up all the potatoes Stan Edgar had just planted. Tex and Stan Edgar both made a grab for him, but Chipshop escaped under the garden shed with a potato in his mouth.

By then I was wishing I could hide under the shed with him, but I had to stand there while Stan Edgar stared me in the face. It made me feel much worse than when *Pasty the Poisoner* had stared at me. I thought, oh, Jelly Jackson, what have you done this time.

I could see he was still angry, but Mr Edgar wasn't shouting any more. He lifted my bag off his potatoes and climbed out of the trench.

'You've had your say,' he said, quite calmly, 'now I'll have mine. You'll never change anyone's opinions by yelling at them. You don't get people to help you that way. Now I suggest you go home and ask your dad, who seems to know so much, if he can't teach you a few manners. Goodbye.' And he held my bag out to me. I couldn't even look him in the face. I took my bag and left. All the others crept out after me.

'And take that thieving animal with you,' Mr Edgar called after us.

Chipshop seemed to know who he was talking about. He crawled out from under the shed, dropped the potato back in the trench and slunk after us with his tail between his legs. If I'd had a tail, that's just where mine would've been too.

Tex was trying not to grin, but he couldn't help himself. 'Ermmm, what was that you were saying before,' he whispered in my ear, 'about Deedee being the one with the temper?'

'Don't start,' I warned him. I knew things hadn't gone to plan and I didn't need Tex to make me feel worse about it. I could have cut my own tongue off. I kept telling myself: you stupid, stupid, *stupid* idiot, you've just blown our last chance!

There was only one thing I was glad about: Zandra hadn't been there to see me do it. That would have given her another good laugh. But when I got home I found out she was probably laughing at me already, her and everyone else in the town. The evening paper had arrived.

eleven

The minute I walked in our Deedee started squawking, 'Da-daaa! Make way for the Media Star. That's if her head'll fit through the door.'

Gav was smiling; Mum and Dad were grinning. They held up the paper to show me the headlines. In big letters it said:

A LOAD OF LOONIES!

Mum read the rest out: *That's what Angelina Jackson and the rest of the netball team at St Stephen's school think of our worthy councillors and their decision to ban competitive sports in schools.*

There was a long piece underneath and a big picture – with me in the middle.

'Look at her,' squealed Deedee. 'She looks like the Incredible Hulk.'

She was right, I did. I could see now what that reporter had been up to. He'd tried to make me look even bigger than I was.

Underneath it said, **CUT OFF IN HER PRIME**. *'They'll be chopping me off at the knees next,'* *says eleven-year-old Angelina. 'It's crazy.'*

'We thought you'd be happy, getting your picture in the paper,' said Dad. But he could tell by my face I wasn't.

'He's made you the star player,' said Mum, trying to cheer me up. 'Written down everything you said.'

'Yeah, every single stupid word,' said Deedee. '*A load of loonies.*' And she kept on reading the same bits out, over and over again.

I didn't dare look at Gav. I could just guess what he was thinking.

Deedee was calling me *Jelly Longlegs*, which she knows I hate. Mum told her to leave me alone, but she just kept stirring it.

'Drop dead,' I said.

'Ewww! I don't know about chopping her legs off, someone should cut her tongue off, before it gets her into any more bother.'

'Mum!' I yelled, 'tell her to stop it.'

But luckily Deedee was running late as usual; she went to get her things together. 'Don't get too comfortable,' she told Gav, 'I need a lift to Kelly's house. We're doing each other a leg wax.' Oh, yuk, I thought.

'You girls certainly know how to have a good time,' Gav laughed.

'We're having a pizza as well,' said Deedee. 'And watching a video. I want you to stop and let me pick one up on the way.'

Honestly! The way she orders Gav about! As usual, he let her get away with it.

'OK,' he said. 'Whenever you're ready.'

I could see my advice last week had gone in one ear and out the other, but I didn't dare say anything. I hadn't exactly followed Gav's advice round at Stan Edgar's myself, or with the newspaper reporter, either.

'Cheer up,' Gav said to me. 'The article could have been worse.'

'Not much,' I said. I tried to explain it wasn't what I'd said.

'Oh, that's what reporters do,' said Dad. 'They make half of it up as they go along.'

But the truth was, the reporter hadn't made it up. It was what I'd said, most of it, it just wasn't what I'd meant.

Later, when Gav had got back from taking Deedee, he came and sat with me, in front of the telly. I wasn't really watching. I was thinking about what I'd said to Stan Edgar and wondering why it was that every time things seemed as if they couldn't get any worse, they did?

And then they got even worse again, 'cos guess whose ugly mug was suddenly all over the TV screen: *Pasty the Poisoner's*. She was on the local news, being interviewed.

The TV reporter was grinning and asking her if

she was one of the *loonies on the council* who was behind this new ban on sports in schools. Gav gave me a nudge, but I just ignored him and stared at the TV.

'Oh,' she laughed, as if it was such a great joke, 'everyone's entitled to their opinion, however...colourfully they express it.'

He asked her what she thought about the campaign to try to prevent the ban. She didn't smile then, she went all serious, looking straight into the camera, and said, 'I feel sure if they really understood why we're doing this, they'd thank us. Believe me, many children will. I still shudder when I remember my own school days: the humiliation of sports lessons, the awful competition, the genuine suffering...'

Oh, boy. She was really putting it on. It wasn't real, you could see that.

'Why would *anyone* vote for her?' I said to Gav.

'Well, lots of people must have. Like I said, it's the ones who get their message across that get elected.'

'Oh, don't start with that *elegant* stuff again!' I begged him.

'Forget about elegant,' said Gav. 'It's about being understood. Making sure you say what you *mean*.' And he waved the newspaper at me, in case I missed his point.

Talk about kicking someone when they're

down. And now I'd gone and done it all over again at Stan Edgar's. I decided to come clean and tell Gav what I'd done – I told him every stupid, embarrassing thing I'd said.

When I'd finished, Gav said, 'Messing up's not a problem, we all do that from time to time. The important thing is to put it right. It's never too late for that.'

I knew he was trying to make me feel better, but it felt too late for me.

When I went to bed I ate a whole packet of lemon jelly cubes before I began to cheer up a bit. When Mum came in to say Goodnight, she said, 'I don't know why you're so glum. You should be very proud of yourself. At least now everybody knows about the ban. You know what they say: no publicity's bad publicity.' I wasn't so sure about that any more.

Later, lying in the dark thinking it all over, I wondered if Gav was right – *again*! At least about Stan Edgar. Perhaps it wasn't too late to put things right with him. There was still a small chance he might help us. It was pretty microscopic, but it had to be worth taking, right?

twelve

I was hoping I might be able to avoid Zandra and Alicia at school on Tuesday morning. I'd already begged everyone else not to tell them what had happened at Stan Edgar's. But before school even started they'd spotted me and Tex walking across the playground. So when Zandra asked me straight out how it had gone, I had to say *something*.

'We didn't really get anywhere. He was a bit of an old grump.'

Zandra shrugged. 'Well, sounds like that's blown our last hope.'

I couldn't argue with that. 'Something else might turn up,' I said.

'Like what?' Zandra snapped. 'A miracle?'

'Miracles happen,' I mumbled, 'sometimes.'

The way Zandra looked at me you'd think I'd just said I still believed in fairies. I could see the others thought I was being a bit weird as well. Even Tex.

Later, when I asked him if he'd come with me to see Stan Edgar again, I don't think he

 82

could believe his ears.

'What on earth for?'

'To try one more time,' I said. 'To change his mind.'

'You mean Stan Edgar's gonna be our miracle?'

'Why not?' I said. 'Stranger things could happen.'

Tex just shook his head and groaned. I knew he'd come with me, though. That's what buddies do, isn't it?

But you see, even without Stan Edgar's help, I was right, something else did turn up. About eleven o'clock we got another message to go straight to Mrs Barker's office again.

This time Mrs Barker wasn't quite so smiley. I don't know why, 'cos it was even better news. She'd had a phone call from the local TV studios. They were only sending a reporter and a cameraman to school to film *us*. For the evening news! Talk about a result! I couldn't resist telling Zandra, 'I told you something would turn up.'

'I wouldn't get too excited,' she said, playing it cool. But I could see she was excited. We all were.

Mrs Barker told us to calm down. She looked like she thought it was getting to be a bit of a nuisance.

'They'll be here in the next hour,' she said, 'so I want you all to go and change into your netball strips. I hope they're clean. Zandra, I know I can rely on you to be sensible. But just in case they want anyone else to speak, we'll have Alicia and...' Mrs Barker looked round for someone else to pick. She sighed, 'Hemma.'

I don't think she could trust anyone else not to put their big fat foot in it, like I'd done last time.

'Now I want you three to speak up clearly. No *umming* and *erring*. Remember everyone at home will see this tonight, our school reputation is resting on you, so I know you'll do your very best.' She didn't seem to realise she was scaring the life out of us.

When Mrs Barker sent everyone else off to get changed, she asked me to wait behind a minute. I thought, oh, no, what's coming now? I didn't dare look at her.

'Just a quick word, Angelina,' she said. 'I'd like *you* to try *not to* speak today. I know you mean well, but I think you said more than enough last time, don't you agree?'

'Yes, Mrs Barker,' I mumbled.

I went out feeling like a squashed tomato. I think my face must have looked the colour of one as well. The thing was, she needn't have said any of that. I'd already decided nothing would get me to open my mouth in front of any kind of reporter ever again.

In the cloakroom everyone was giggling and saying how nervous they were feeling. Zandra was combing her hair and asking Alicia, 'Do you think I should tie it in a ponytail or leave it loose?'

Maxine asked me what Mrs Barker'd wanted, but I just shook my head, as if it was nothing, and started getting changed.

Miss Summers came to find us when she heard the news.

'I'm so proud of you all,' she said, beaming at us. 'See what you started, Jelly. This is all because of you and your petition.' That made me feel a little better. I don't think Zandra liked it, though. She gave me a bit of a slit-eyed look.

Tex skived off and came and sat with us while we waited for the TV people to arrive. He whispered to me, 'I think Mrs Barker should've chosen you to do the talking. I would've done.'

'Well, she didn't, did she?' Zandra started up. 'She chose us, because she knows we won't say anything stupid. Or use bad language. Or lose our temper. Or get people's names wrong.'

'At least Jelly wouldn't play with her hair and go on about her dancing career,' said Maxine. That shut Zandra up, for a second at least.

'Just remember this is about *netball*,' Abi warned Zandra.

Zandra said, 'If you think any of you could do any better...'

'I bet Jelly could, *actually*,' said Tex. 'Don't

forget the petition was her idea in the first place.'

'And don't you forget this is netball business, nothing to do with you,' Zandra told Tex. 'So I suggest you just keep out of it.'

I thought, here we go. Why are we fighting so hard to save this team, when we don't even behave like one? If we don't stop bickering and start pulling together, this minute, there won't be a team to save anyway. So, I told them, 'Pack in squabbling, all of you. Stop picking on Zandra. She *is* better with words than the rest of us. That's why Mrs Barker chose her. She'll do her best.' But when I saw the smug look on Zandra's face, I could have swallowed the words right back down again.

As it turned out none of us got to hear what Zandra said, because we were all sent to play netball in the background, while Zandra talked to the reporter in front of the camera. They took ages checking sound levels and moving her into different positions. Mrs Barker was there as well, fussing and chasing off infants who were trying to get their faces on TV. I think Mrs Barker expected to be interviewed too, but the reporter told her the reason this was such a good story was because it'd all come from the kids. Which was true, even if Zandra was the only one who was getting her face on the telly in the end.

After they'd left we tried to find out what

Zandra'd said, but she got really ratty and told us she couldn't exactly remember.

'It wasn't easy having a microphone stuck in my face,' she snapped. 'I did my best. You'll just have to watch it on TV tonight.'

'Get her!' said Maxine. 'The TV Star.'

'Can I have your autograph?' said Tex.

'She'll be wanting her own chat show next,' said Abi.

'Singing and dancing,' Hemma joined in.

Zandra went off in a temper. She can't bear to be teased.

'I think she got a bit nervous,' Alicia told us.

'Oh, no, I hope she didn't blow it,' said Maxine.

'I'm glad I didn't have to do it,' said Hemma.

I knew what Hemma meant. If anyone had blown it, I was just glad this time it wasn't me.

The rest of the day went past in a bit of a blur. We couldn't wait to get home and see our moment of fame on TV. Boy, were we in for a disappointment.

But before that I had to find Mum and tell her I'd be a bit late getting home. I had something important to do. I wasn't looking forward to it one little bit. And neither was Tex. He was all for waiting a couple of days, to give Stan Edgar chance to calm down, until I reminded him that in a couple of days it would all be too late.

thirteen

When we got to Stan Edgar's house for the second time, his wife said, 'Oh, it's you again, is it? Well, you can come in, but you'll have to wait until *Countdown*'s finished.'

We were going to leave Chipshop at the gate, but she told us we could bring him in. I didn't think that was such a good idea, after his tricks yesterday, but it was starting to rain. Tex got hold of Chipshop's collar and hissed in his ear that he could have his chew but he had to be on his best behaviour, or else. Chipshop looked up at us as if dog chocs wouldn't melt in his mouth. Yeah, right.

When we went into the lounge Stan Edgar didn't even take his eyes off the telly. For the next quarter of an hour no one made a sound, apart from Chipshop with his chew and Mr Edgar shouting out the answers. He was really good, he got most of 'em right.

Tex said, 'You should go on this programme, Mr Edgar, I bet you'd win.' But he still didn't look at us. I was wondering what had ever made me think it was a good idea to come back.

When the programme was over, Mrs Edgar said she'd make us all a cup of tea. I started looking round the room while we waited. There were photographs everywhere, some of their family, but most were of Stan Edgar standing with groups of men, or shaking hands with people, or holding banners in marches. There were one or two with him waving his arms, grinning like he'd won the lottery. He was a lot younger, but you could still tell it was him.

Mrs Edgar offered us some more of those chocolate biscuits and it was starting to feel like we'd come round for a tea party, until Mr Edgar suddenly said to me, 'Now, then, young lady, have you come back to give me another duffing up or to eat some humble pie?' I nearly choked on my biscuit. 'Let's hear what you've got to say, then, and this time you don't have to shout. I may be old and past it but I'm not completely deaf.'

This time I knew I'd gotta get it right, so I took a deep breath and started. 'I didn't mean to shout at you,' I said. 'I'm really sorry. It's just 'cos it's so important. It came out all wrong. It does that sometimes, when I get worked up,' I admitted.

Then I told him why netball's the best thing in the world, and all about the league, and how hard Miss Summers had worked, and all about the petition, and trying to give it to Mrs Barker and then to Patsy Poysner, and how horrible she'd been, and all about getting her name wrong and calling her *Pasty Poisoner* on the envelope... He nearly spilled his tea when I told him that bit!

And all about the newspaper reporter, and the TV crew. Everything. I knew I was gabbling, but there was so much to get in. When I'd finished I held out the petition. 'I know I shouldn't have lost my temper, but, please, will you take this to the council for us? *Please?*'

Mr Edgar didn't answer me for a minute. Then he said, 'Well, you've been big enough to admit you were wrong and I'm not too old to do the same. I could have listened to you with a bit more respect. But I did try to tell you this was *out of my hands*. And, before you have another tantrum,' he said quickly, 'sometimes you have to accept that's just how it is. Like I told you yesterday, I think it's too late. As far as forgiving you's concerned...I'll have to think about that. '

I was so gutted I nearly started shouting again. But I didn't want to blow it. So I said, quite quietly, 'Gav says it's never too late – if you really care about something. He says there's always something you can do.'

'Is that right?' Stan Edgar looked a bit surprised. 'And who's Gav when he's at home?'

I surprised myself a bit when I said, 'He's

a friend of mine.'

'Well, tell Gav, it's not bad advice, on the whole, but on this occasion I think he may be wrong. I will deliver the petition for you, though, I can do that at least.'

Before we left, Stan Edgar picked up his newspaper. There I was, staring out from the picture, looking like a telegraph pole. My heart just fell into my trainers, but he smiled for the first time since we'd arrived. He picked up one of his photographs. It was of a young lad in jeans and a leather jacket. Two policemen were carrying him by his arms and legs. He looked really mad. I thought, that can't be Stan Edgar. But it was.

'I was just like you when I was younger,' he said, pointing to the photo, 'spoke first and thought after. It got me in a lot of bother, as you can see. But you'll learn.'

As we were going through the front door, Mr Edgar shouted after us. 'I think you've forgotten something,' and suddenly Chipshop raced past us with a slipper in his mouth. Mr Edgar was right behind him.

'That's one thieving dog you've got there,' he said, grabbing his slipper. Chipshop wasn't bothered. He jumped up for a stroke, but Mr Edgar said, 'Don't push your luck, Muttley,' whoever Muttley is.

'I don't think Mr Edgar likes dogs,' I told Tex as we walked home.

'I think he likes you though,' said Tex.

I don't know how Tex worked that out. Even if he did, a fat lot of good it had done us. 'Looks like this is where we finally give up,' I said.

'Are you mad?' said Tex. 'Give up, after all you've done? No way.'

'You heard him,' I said, 'we've lost. Might as well forget it.'

'What about that miracle?' Tex reminded me.

'Humph,' I said. 'Only kids believe in miracles.'

When I was nearly home I heard a van backfiring and Evie came round the corner. Gav slowed down and wound his window down.

'You're late coming home,' he said.

So I told him that we'd been back to see Stan Edgar and exactly what I'd said to him. 'Good for you,' Gav said. 'Sounds as if you did pretty well at explaining yourself. I'm proud of you, *mon ami*. You're turning into a real little fighter.'

'Less of the little,' I said. After all, I was nearly as big as Gav. Then I told him about us being on TV, as well.

'You've had quite a day, haven't you?' he laughed. 'I'd better give you a lift home after all that.'

But as things turned out, that wasn't such

a good move. Deedee was on the warpath. Big time.

'Where do you think you've been?' she shouted at Gav.

'I just met Jelly and we got talking,' he said.

'I'm going to be late for Aerobics, again,' Deedee yelled.

'I'm here now,' said Gav, dead calmly. 'I'll go and start the van.'

But Deedee didn't follow him.

'What's the point of him hanging round here all the time,' she yelled at me, 'if when I really I need him he's running round after you?!'

'He just bumped into me round the corner,' I told her. 'That's all.' Then I started to tell Mum about the TV people, but Deedee cut me off.

'I'm sick of you,' she said. 'You think you rule this house. You and your precious netball. And now you've got Gav as daft about it as you.'

Mum reminded Deedee she was late already and that Gav was waiting outside in the van, but Deedee didn't care.

'Good,' she said. 'Now *he* can do the waiting.'

How stupid was that? She was the one who was gonna be late for her evening class, not Gav.

'Well, that's it,' she said. 'I'm gonna give him an ultimatum. I'm gonna tell him he can choose: her and her silly little mates or me. It's up to him. I don't care one way or the other.' Then she went flouncing out. Mum shook her head.

I said, 'She's nothing but a user, the way she treats Gav.'

Mum gave me a bit of a look and said, 'Gav's too soft for his own good. It seems to me we all take advantage of his kind nature.'

I could tell she meant me as well. And she was right. Lately I'd been expecting Gav to listen to me moaning on, and run me about all over the place as well. I was no better than Deedee. That left me feeling a bit funny, I can tell you.

When Gav got back from dropping Deedee off, I tried to tell him how grateful I was for all the lifts and all his help and all the chats. I think I laid it on a bit thick.

'Yeah, yeah, I know,' he said, waving me away.

He didn't look like someone who'd just had a big ultimatum. I was dying to find out what Deedee'd said to him, but before I could ask he said, 'Aren't we going to watch the news?'

I couldn't believe I'd forgotten all about it. I grabbed the remote.

'Mum! Mum!' I yelled. 'Quick, I'm on the telly.'

fourteen

It was lucky Gav was there to remember to put a tape in the video.

'Oh, yes, Dad won't want to miss it,' said Mum.

'Or Deedee,' said Gav.

I thought, as if she cares, unless I'd fallen over mid-shot and broken my leg, then she'd have had a good laugh.

Suddenly it was on and there we all were, the whole netball team. It felt so weird seeing myself on TV. Not that we were on long. Even Gav had to admit if you'd blinked you'd have missed us.

It started with a close up of us playing: Zandra passing to Abi, Abi to Maxine, Maxine to me and just as I was about to take the shot, can you believe it, they cut straight to the reporter! They chopped my goal! Talk about missing the action!

The reporter was explaining about the council's ban when Zandra ran over to join him, so she missed him getting her name wrong!

'But the netball team at St Stephen's School have decided to tackle the council head on,' he said. 'Sandra Andrews, captain of the team, is here with me now.'

The reporter asked Zandra to tell him about the petition. She started off OK, but she didn't mention the council stopping the insurance. In fact she didn't tell him much. She kept playing with her hair and doing all that *umming* and *erring* Mrs Barker told her not to do.

Then, even though we'd warned her not to, she just couldn't resist it: 'It's not quite as bad for me,' she said, 'because I have other interests...' I thought, please don't say it, but she did, '...like dancing. I once auditioned, you know, for *Les Miserables...*'

Oh, boy, I thought, wait till Hemma and Maxine get you tomorrow. The whole thing was over in a minute and a half. I couldn't believe it.

Mum said, 'Wasn't that great. Wait 'til your dad sees it. You all looked smashing. And didn't Zandra do well.'

I looked at Gav and he rolled his eyes.

Later, when Mum went to do some ironing, we watched it all over again. It took longer to find the bit on the tape than it did to watch it.

Zandra seemed even more hopeless the second time round.

'Why on earth did she get picked instead of you?' Gav asked me.

I nearly burst out laughing. 'Because Zandra always gets picked. Because she's prettier and cleverer and she doesn't shoot her mouth off. And she's Mrs Barker's favourite. Anyway, I don't care.'

'Well, you should,' Gav told me. 'Zandra might be cleverer as far as schoolwork goes, but there're different ways of being clever, *mon ami*. I've told you before; you're more talented than you think you are. Look at how well you did today at Stan Edgar's house, that's proof enough.'

Fat lot of good it's done us, I thought.

'Admit it,' Gav went on, 'You know you could have done better. If you weren't too scared to try.'

'Scared?! I'm not scared,' I said, jumping up, ready for a scrap.

Gav burst out laughing. 'I'd never noticed before,' he said, 'but just then you didn't half look like your sister.'

Yuk. I hoped he was wrong about that. It was enough to give a girl nightmares.

Anyway he had some nerve calling me a scaredy-cat. A minute later, when his mobile rang, he scuttled off again to pick up The Queen of Sheba. I knew he was never gonna stand up to Deedee, no matter what I said to him.

I was getting into my pyjamas when they came home. I could tell they were watching the tape because Deedee was laughing like a hyena. I don't know why I went downstairs – I knew she'd wind me up.

'Is that it?' Deedee said when it was finished.

'Famous for half a second. Did they have to cut your shot 'cos you missed?'

'No,' I told her, 'I never miss.'

'Ewww! I told you it'd all go to her head. My sister the TV star.'

Gav was grinning at me and when Deedee caught me grinning back she really went off on one, 'I don't know what you think's so funny. I'm sick of you two ganging up against me.'

She was being so stupid Gav burst out laughing, but that only wound her up even more. 'I'm sick of you. Why don't you go home?' she told him, stamping her foot like a four year old. 'And don't bother coming back!'

Then she went off to her bedroom to play her music dead loud.

Seeing Gav looking so sorry for himself, half of me wanted to shake him, but the other half wanted to cheer him up. I thought, time for another heart to heart.

'Gav, what d'you see in our Deedee?' I asked him. 'I really don't get it?'

'You don't choose who you fall for,' he said, blushing. 'It just happens. You'll find out one day.'

I thought, you're wrong there, mate.

'But she's such an idiot,' I said. 'And you're not. Most of the time.'

'Gee, thanks.' Gav grinned at me. 'I suppose it's a chemistry thing. It's how someone makes you feel. It makes me happy just to see her. She's pretty and funny and...full of life.'

I thought, I know what Deedee's full of, but I'm not supposed to use language like that. 'Sometimes she wants a good slap,' I said.

Gav laughed. 'She's got a temper, for sure, but underneath that I reckon she's just a bit scared.'

'Scared?! Our Deedee?! She's sixteen, for goodness sake.'

'So?' Gav said. 'Most of the time when people lose their temper it's because they're frightened. Adults as well.'

'Frightened of what?'

'Anything. Everything. You'd be surprised.'

'Did I just say you *weren't* an idiot?' I said. 'Well, I take it back.'

Gav laughed again and shrugged. 'You know what the French say?' No, I thought, but you're gonna tell me. '*Vive la difference!*'

'Which means?'

'You know, it's good to be different. Male/female, black/white, tall/short, noisy/quiet. If we were all the same, how dull would that be?'

That made me think about the netball ban again. That's just what that was about, trying to make us all the same instead of admitting everyone's different – and good at different things.

Sometimes, though, I wished Deedee wasn't

quite so different. Things'd be quieter round our house at least.

When I went up to bed, there was a heavy thudding sound coming from Deedee's bedroom. There was no chance I was getting to sleep any time soon, so I made a tent under the duvet and tried to think. It looked like it really was all over. Between us we'd blown all our chances. *Pasty the Poisoner* was our big enemy now, Stan Edgar wasn't exactly on our side. The newspaper article had landed me in Mrs Barker's bad books and Zandra had blown our big chance on TV.

Gav seemed to think I'd have done the TV interview better than Zandra, but he was wrong. Wasn't I the one that'd messed up all the other times? I had to face it, there was only one thing I was any good at: netball. I was the Shooting Star. It was my only bit of magic. So I'd better stick to that, for as long as we'd got it, which reminded me – tomorrow was Wednesday and that meant our last practice – *ever*!

fifteen

When we got to school next morning we got mobbed in the playground. Loads of kids started asking for our autographs. You'd think we'd been on *Pop Idol* or something. I told you Maxine and Hemma would be fizzing mad with Zandra and they were. By break time they weren't speaking to each other. When I tried to get them to sign a thank you card for Miss Summers that Mum had given me that morning, Maxine and Hemma wouldn't put their names on the same side of the card as Zandra's. How stupid was that?

Then, about half an hour before lunchtime, we got *another* message for all of us to go to Mrs Barker's office.

'This is getting ridiculous,' said Abi.

'What d'you think it's about this time?' Zandra asked Alicia. She was deliberately not speaking to the rest of us.

'Perhaps it's Hollywood, wanting to make a film,' Abi started up, 'starring you and Alicia...'

'*Dancing*,' said Hemma and Maxine together.

Zandra gave them a nasty look. The truth

was none of us could guess what it was about this time. And Mrs Barker's face wasn't giving anything away.

'Well,' she said, sighing. 'The good news is: there's been an invitation for you all to go to the Town Hall. It seems the council members want to hear your arguments against the competitive sports ban.'

We were all gob-smacked. We weren't expecting that.

Then she hit us with the bad news. 'The meeting's tomorrow at three thirty, which doesn't leave you much time to prepare.'

'Tomorrow!' we gasped. We could hardly believe it.

'Try not to get your hopes up. This doesn't mean anything's going to change,' she said. 'But I suppose you've done well to get this far.'

There must be a chance, though, I thought, if they even want to hear what we've got to say. The idea of having to talk in front of the whole council was mega-scary. *I* wouldn't have fancied that one little bit. But I needn't have worried. Mrs Barker had other ideas.

'Zandra's the obvious person to speak on your behalf,' she said.

'But the petition was Jelly's idea in the first place,' said Maxine. Mrs Barker looked at Maxine as if she'd said something really stupid. Then she eyeballed me. 'It's important we choose someone who can put the arguments across, *in appropriate language*,' she said. I just looked down at the floor. I was glad she'd chosen Zandra anyway. I didn't want the job. 'But you'll need to work together on it,' Mrs Barker told us. 'I know I can rely on you to do that.' We all smiled nervously, as if we were having our photo taken. 'Come and show me when you've got something worked out.'

Mrs Barker hadn't told us whose idea it had been to invite us to the council meeting. Tex said it was nothing to do with his dad this time. He felt sure it was Stan Edgar, but Stan Edgar hadn't looked like he was on our side to me.

Anyway the important thing was: we'd got another chance – this time we had to make it count.

After lunch Miss Summers said we could all go to the library, where it was quiet, to work on a list of the reasons why the council should change their minds.

OK, some of our ideas were better than others. But every time it was Maxine or Abi's suggestion, Zandra sniggered and said, 'Oh, that will really convince them. *Not*.'

And whenever Zandra made a suggestion Maxine and Hemma rolled their eyes and yawned as if they were too bored to live.

I was starting to feel like I was refereeing a boxing match.

'We're a team,' I reminded them. 'That's how we always win – by teamwork, which should be the main reason on our list.'

Nobody argued with that, but they were all still itching for a fight.

When we showed the list to Mrs Barker, she said they were all good reasons. Now we had to put them into a short speech for Zandra to learn.

'Learn?' Zandra looked completely freaked.

'You can use your list as a reminder, but you need to work out exactly what you're going to say,' Mrs Barker told Zandra. 'To get your points across clearly and convincingly.' It was the kind of stuff Gav'd been telling me. 'Tonight you can learn it, then tomorrow morning you can practise it on your friends. They'll help you get it really polished.'

I saw Maxine and Hemma smirking when Mrs Barker called us Zandra's friends. I gave them both a hard stare. This was too important to mess up, just because they were acting like a pair of infants.

We trooped back to the library to start again. Tex had been pestering Miss Summers to let him come and help us, but he only made matters worse. He and Maxine started fooling around – writing on each other's hands, and silly stuff like that.

'OK,' said Zandra, like she was the teacher. 'Let's get on with it.'

'Yes, Miss. Sorry, Miss,' said Tex, in a silly voice. Oh, boy, I could see trouble brewing.

It had been quite easy coming up with the reasons against the ban, but trying to decide exactly what Zandra should say wasn't. We went round in circles.

'I think it'll be easier if you just leave this to me,' she said finally.

'So you can bang on again,' said Maxine, 'about...'

'...*dancing, dancing, dancing...*' all of them, apart from me and Alicia, started singing, and making little dancing steps with their fingers on the table.

Well, that was it. Zandra went red in the face. 'I'd like to see how far you'd get without Alicia and me.'

'We don't need you,' said Abi. 'Jelly can do it.'

'Oh, yes,' said Zandra. 'It should go down very well when she calls the councillors *loony* and *crazy*. That should really win them round.'

'At least she won't bore everyone to death,' said Hemma quietly.

'Well, good luck to her,' Zandra said, storming out of the library, dragging Alicia with her. 'Let's leave them to it.'

The others looked so pleased: Maxine and Abi and Tex were doing a victory wave. I couldn't believe them.

'Now you've done it,' I said. 'I hope you're

proud of yourselves.'

'You can take over now,' said Maxine.

'We thought you'd be pleased,' said Tex.

'Do I look pleased?' I said.

We had less than an hour before hometime.

Half an hour later, when Mrs Barker came to see how we were getting on, there wasn't much to show her. She sent me to find Zandra and Alicia to ask them to come back. Zandra looked so smug, but after Mrs Barker'd finished giving us all a good roasting, no one was smiling.

'You've got just twenty minutes left before hometime,' she told us. 'If you haven't finished by then you may need to stay behind after school.'

'But it's our last netball practice,' Abi told her. 'We can't miss that.'

'Then, I suggest you get a move on.'

After that they all looked fit to kill each other. I sat on one side of the table with Zandra and Alicia; the rest of the team sat on the other. I could tell they thought I was taking Zandra's side, but if I hadn't done something to keep the peace we wouldn't have got anywhere. As it was we hadn't got much further when the bell went. The minute they heard it the others leapt out of their seats. Zandra shook her head as if to say, isn't that just typical.

'We haven't finished yet,' she said.

'Yeah, but it's netball practice,' said Maxine.

'Personally, I don't see the point of a last practice,' she said to Alicia. 'I'm not sure why we're bothering.'

'Don't bother, then,' said Maxine. 'We won't miss you.'

'Good riddance,' said Abi.

They all went off then and left me there with Zandra and Alicia.

I could see Zandra was waiting for me to say something nasty as well, but I wasn't looking for a fight. I knew we needed the two of them to have a proper practice. And I was sure they didn't really want to miss the very last one. But Zandra wasn't one for backing down. And I wasn't one for grovelling.

Suddenly I knew what to say. It was as if Gav was sitting on my shoulder.

'Listen, Zandra,' I said, 'I know there doesn't seem much point to anything at the moment. But think how upset Miss Summers'll be if you two don't come, after all the work she's put in.'

Zandra and Alicia looked at each other and sighed. I knew straight away I'd got them.

'Don't worry,' Zandra said, snootily. 'We wouldn't dream of letting Miss Summers down, would we, Alicia? Some of us understand the meaning of loyalty!' I couldn't stop myself smiling and she saw me. 'And some of us can spell it,' she added.

Oh, miaow! I thought. But I just let it go. I was definitely learning there were better ways to crack a nut than with a hammer. Gav would've been so proud of me.

sixteen

Netball practice started really badly. We always wipe the floor with the second team; today they were beating us. Knowing this was our last practice, you'd think we'd have wanted to make the most of it, wouldn't you? But the arguments in the team were really beginning to show. Hemma wouldn't pass to Zandra and the odd times Zandra got the ball she wouldn't pass to Abi or Hemma or Maxine, which made it a pretty useless game. Miss Summers looked so disappointed with us.

At half-time when we changed ends I couldn't keep quiet any longer. 'Look, if this is our last game, d'you want it to be the worst we've ever played? D'you want to let Miss Summers down that badly? For goodness' sake,' I said, 'stop acting like a load of spoilt brats.'

'Charmingly put,' said Zandra.

'Don't start on that,' I warned her.

'You tell her, Jelly,' said Maxine.

'And you can zip it,' I said. 'You're as bad as each other. Either play like a team or let's all go home now.'

Everyone looked dead shocked, but it seemed to work. They came out and played as if it mattered. And we hammered the second team 30-15. For the first time in ages I wasn't thinking about the ban. Or what might happen tomorrow at the council. I was just concentrating on being the team's *Shooting Star*.

After the practice Miss Summers took me to one side and told me again how proud of me she was.

'Now, how are you all getting to the Town Hall tomorrow?' she asked. 'I could take a few in my car, but it won't fit everyone in.'

I told her it was fine. I was going to ask Gav; he'd helped us out the other time. I knew he'd want to take us, when he heard about it.

'Well, make sure you're all looking smart. Don't let us down.'

'We won't, Miss,' I promised her.

When the others asked me what she'd been saying, I only told them about the lift and looking smart tomorrow.

'Well, I'm not wearing *my* best clothes,' Zandra whispered to Alicia, 'not if we're going in that rust bucket again.'

She didn't think I'd heard, but I had.

'Why is it, every time we start behaving like a team again, someone has to go and spoil it?' I asked Tex as we walked home.

'Zandra's jealous, 'cos you're a better player,' he said. 'And Miss Summers likes you more.'

'She does not,' I said.

'She does too. She'd make you captain now if it wasn't for the ban.'

'She only said that to be nice.'

'Today she said you were the star player. That you were *amazing*.'

I knew that bit could've been true, 'cos today I had been playing well. I could feel it. But I still didn't believe the bit about clever-clogs Zandra being jealous of me. *Me* – the tall, gawky thick one! That made no sense. Sometimes Tex talks as much rubbish as Gav.

'I can't wait to tell my dad about tomorrow,' Tex said, as he turned into his road. 'He'll be dead chuffed. I bet he'll come and support us.'

'It's not like it's a netball match,' I shouted after him.

'Whatever,' Tex called back. 'Just make sure you get Gav the Taxi booked, otherwise we're stuffed.'

When I got home Mum wasn't in from work, but Dad and Gav were in the lounge watching the telly.

'Guess what?' I said, throwing my bag down.

'I think we might need a little clue,' said Gav.

'The whole netball team's been invited to the

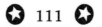 111

Town Hall tomorrow. To talk to the council.'

Gav was all smiles. 'Good for you. The revolution goes on!'

'What revolution?' said Dad.

'*Against the netball ban!* I said. 'They want to hear all our arguments.'

'Politicians wanting to hear what someone else has got to say? I'll believe that when I see it,' said Dad.

'Tex says *his* dad'll come and support us,' I told him.

'Oh, he would. His dad's into all that.'

I felt a bit cross with Dad, pouring cold water all over my good news. But Gav was excited for me.

'Well, I think it's great,' he said. 'And who knows, maybe you will change their minds. So have you got to give a speech?'

'Not me,' I said.

Gav groaned. 'Oh, Jelly. Not Zandra? How did that happen?'

'It wasn't up to me,' I almost shouted at him.

'Big mistake,' said Gav. 'Well, you'll just have to coach her. Help her put some heart into the message.'

I looked at him like he was talking Chinese this time.

'Oh, yeah, I can really see Zandra listening to me,' I said.

'You'll have to *make* her listen,' said Gav. 'Use your new powers of persuasion. You've had plenty of practice lately.'

Which reminds me, I thought...time to get a bit more practice in. 'Ga-a-av,' I said, trying to turn on the charm, like our Deedee does, 'would you be able to take us to the Town Hall tomorrow in your van? Pretty ple-ea-se?'

'Of course. No need to actually grovel, though,' Gav said, grinning.

But before I could say thanks, the door flew open and Deedee came bursting in with some good news of her own.

I didn't realise at first what a close thing it had been. I'd got our lift booked in the nick of time.

seventeen

Boy, was Deedee in a good mood. She'd just heard she'd got an interview for that job on the fashion magazine. She was wiggling her bottom and saying, 'Who's a clever girl, then?'

Nobody was bothered about my news any more.

'I really want this job,' she said. 'It's what I've been waiting for.'

'You'll get it,' said Gav, grinning. 'You'll do it easy.'

'And how do you know?' she said, batting her eyelids at him. 'How do you know what I can do?'

He went all red then and didn't know what to say. I dunno, Gav the Dictionary lost for words. Pathetic, eh!

Mum had come home by then so Deedee showed her the letter.

'The interview's tomorrow,' she said, 'so I'll have to get everything organised tonight. And decide what to wear. And do my hair.'

Then she went into this big number about how she had nothing to wear. Even though her wardrobe's so full she can't close the doors.

'Jelly's got some news as well,' Dad said, before he left for work.

Mum'd already heard, from *The-One-Who-Must-Be-Obeyed* – Mrs Barker. But Deedee hadn't, so Gav told her all about it.

She said, 'Going into politics as well now? Is there no end to her talents?' She did manage a smile, though.

Wow! I thought, she must be in a good mood. But it didn't last long. Five minutes in fact. Just until Mum asked me how we were all getting to the Town Hall tomorrow, and I said, 'Gav says he's—'

I didn't even get to finish my sentence before Deedee went into orbit.

'Oh no, he isn't,' she screamed, like she was at a pantomime. 'It's my interview tomorrow afternoon and that's more important than you and your silly netball team.'

Dad tried to sort things out. 'I'll get up early and take you,' he told her.

But that wasn't good enough for Deedee. 'That's not the point,' she said. 'This is a matter of principle.' Whatever that meant.

Dad waved his hands as much as to say, OK, leave me out of it. 'I'm off to work,' he said. Mum shook her head. She could see what was coming next.

Gav had gone silent on us, the coward.

'Gav, you *promised*,' I begged him. 'We need the van to fit us all in. There's only one of Deedee. We're depending on you to get us there.'

'I don't believe this,' said Deedee, standing right in front of Gav, daring him to cross her. 'Gav, tell her.'

Gav took this slow, deep breath. He looked at Deedee, then back at me, and I just knew who he was gonna choose. I thought, you call yourself a friend, *mon ami*! but the minute Deedee shouts jump! you jump. You're still Gav the Doormat! I was so sure he was gonna let me down, I nearly passed out when he said, 'Well, I did promise Jelly before you came in. Sorry, Deedee. The Revolution needs me.'

I thought Deedee was gonna explode.

'*The Revolution needs you?!* What about me?! You hang around here like it's your second home, trying to get round me, but lately when *I* really want *you* you're never here. I used to think you were the kind of person who kept their promises.'

'I do, I am—' Gav tried to chip in, but Deedee wasn't gonna be interrupted.

'These days you seem to be more interested in hanging out with *her*,' she said, making me sound as if I was something the cat had dragged in! 'Well, it's ultimatum time,' she said suddenly. 'I just want to know who you really want to go out with, Gav – me or my eleven-year-old kid sister?!

Because I'm beginning to wonder.'

I could feel this laugh getting bigger inside me and it was about to burst out when Mum suddenly grabbed me and pulled me into the kitchen. She didn't quite close the door, though. We were hugging each other, dying to laugh, but Mum put her finger to my lips to stop me. She didn't want us to miss Gav's answer to the big ultimatum.

It had all gone quiet in the lounge, like Gav was really having to think it over. Then we heard him say, 'Hmmm, tough choice, Deedee.' He sounded so laid back, so Mr Cool. 'I think I'll have to get back to you on that one. See ya tomorrow.'

Then we heard him leave, closing the front door behind him. There was a sort of strangled cry from Deedee, then the sound of her feet stamping up the stairs and her bedroom door banging. Really loud!

Mum and me peeped out of the kitchen and when I'd checked the coast was clear I raced outside after Gav. I saw him disappearing down the road.

'I'm proud of you, *mon ami*,' I called after him. 'I really think there's hope for you yet!'

Gav smiled and waved back. Who'd have thought it, Gav the Hero after all.

When I went back inside I headed straight upstairs to lie on my bed to think things over. *And* to keep out of Deedee's way. What a day it had been! For the past two weeks, since the netball ban, something different had happened every day. And every time, when there was something good – like the newspaper or the TV interview – hot on its heels came another disaster. Like Deedee tonight. But I'd won that battle. We'd got the lift.

We still had the biggest battle to come, though: convincing the council they'd made a mistake. That was up to Zandra now. I thought about her at home, trying to finish the speech all on her own. And then she'd got to learn it by heart. I was so glad it wasn't me.

That thing Gav had said, what was it...*Vive La Difference!* was dead right: we *are* all different. I thought, Zandra is the right one to do the speech, that's why Mrs Barker chose her. She was the only one clever enough. OK, she might not speak from her heart, but at least she wouldn't talk out of her bottom, which I'd probably end up doing. And I didn't think that'd go down very well with the councillors now, would it?

Shooting goals was my thing and I should stick to that. I'd done too much shooting my mouth off lately, and I didn't know why Gav couldn't see that.

eighteen

It was our big day at last and I didn't even want to get out of bed. I know I should have felt excited, but I was just scared. I thought of that joke that Tex likes so much: What lies at the bottom of the ocean, shivering? A nervous wreck. That was me.

For once I was glad we've got a school uniform 'cos it meant I didn't have to worry about what to wear. Mum had put out a clean sweatshirt so I looked quite smart – from the neck down. But my hair was doing its own thing as usual. Mum had just finished fighting with it to get it into two bunches.

'What does your hair look like?' Deedee snorted when she came downstairs all dolled up ready for her interview. I just glared at her and reached for the cereal. But she snatched the packet first. I didn't care, I felt too sick to eat anyway. But Mum had seen her.

'Deedee, don't start a fight this morning, please,' she said. 'You've both got a big day ahead.'

That was all it needed to get Deedee going. 'Me start a fight?! She's the one that started it in the first place. If it wasn't for her Gav would be taking me to my interview—'

'We've been over this,' said Mum, cutting her off. 'Your interview's at two o'clock. Gav's got plenty of time to take you and drop you off before he collects Jelly and her friends.'

'Forget it. After last night I wouldn't ask him for a lift if I had two broken legs.'

'Oh, *please*,' I said. 'Do we have to have the Drama Queen routine.'

'And you can tell him from me when you see him not to come round here again.'

'Tell him yourself,' I snapped. 'He's your boyfriend.'

'He is *not* my *boyfriend*,' she screamed. 'He never has been my boyfriend and he never will be my boyfriend. I don't want to speak to him ever again!' Then she stormed off upstairs, shouting, 'Thanks to you.'

'She's nervous, that's all,' said Mum.

Nervous? I thought. I was nervous; she was hysterical.

When I got to school some of the others were talking about how their mums and dads had promised to try to get time off work to come to the Town Hall to support us. I knew Mum couldn't be there, Mrs Barker'd never give her time off, and Dad would be in bed, 'cos of his shifts, so I felt a bit left out and let down, 'specially when Tex said all his dad's mates were coming as well. With placards! Tex said he'd even made a banner for Chipshop to wear saying: *Save Our Netball!*

'That sounds so stupid,' said Zandra. 'Like someone's run off with the ball.'

'They might as well have,' said Tex.

When they asked me if Gav was taking us in his van, I just said yes. I didn't tell them how much trouble it had caused at home. I felt bad enough thinking Gav might have thrown away his chances with Deedee for ever, just to help us out. I tried not to think about *that*. We still had the speech to sort out.

But when I asked Zandra if it was finished, and how she was feeling, she almost bit my ear off. It was like being back at home with Deedee.

'I don't need you or anybody else checking up on me, thank you very much, Jelly Jackson. I know what I'm doing, OK?!'

'I was only trying to help,' I said. And I backed off while I still had two ears left.

I knew Zandra must be feeling nervous, but it seemed odd for her to be that uptight. She's usually pretty full of herself. Once or twice I looked over at her in class, and tried to give her a friendly sort of smile, but she just froze me to the spot so I gave up. I told the others, if she's got it under control, perhaps we should just leave her to it.

Later, when Mrs Barker came to check up on us, and asked us if the speech was finished, Zandra just nodded. We had to go along with it. We weren't gonna snitch on her. Then there was nothing else to do, except wait for three o'clock. It seemed a long day thanks to Abi – giving us time checks every ten minutes. She'd suddenly turned into the talking clock.

A minute after three we were all standing at the school gates waiting for Gav. Zandra was looking like Deedee in a facemask – raised from the dead. But there was nothing we could do to help. I was finally starting to feel excited and I couldn't wait for Gav's van to turn the corner.

Even before we saw Evie we heard her a couple of roads away, sounding more like a tank than ever. Miss Summers looked a bit worried, but I told her, 'Don't worry, Miss, she's just an old lady. Her rattle's worse than her bite.'

When Evie finally came round the corner everyone burst out cheering. Gav had tied ribbons and flags to her and a few balloons. Along the side was a big banner saying:

VIVE LA REVOLUTION!

Miss Summers smiled, but over the noise of the van she shouted, 'I think I'd better take some of you in my car, just in case. Zandra, you and Alicia can come with me. Wait here and I'll drive round and collect you.'

While Miss Summers went to bring her car, Gav opened the back doors of the van for everyone to get in. I thought I'd sit in the front with Gav this time. I was just going to open the front door when Zandra grabbed hold of my arm. I mean, hard enough to pull it off. She looked terrible.

Her face was the colour of porridge. And then it came – another big bombshell.

'Jelly, I can't go through with this,' she said, pushing a folded piece of paper into my hand. 'Here, you'll have to do it.' Then she ran off to get into Miss Summers' car.

I must have stood there for ages, like I'd been turned to stone, 'cos then I realised Gav was tapping on the window and asking me what I was waiting for. In the end he opened the door and nearly dragged me inside.

'What's up?' he said. 'You look like you're off to the torture chamber.'

That's exactly what I felt like. Everyone else was in the back of the van, singing and laughing, but I just wanted to go home and hide under my bed.

'Zandra's bottled out,' I whispered. 'She says I've got to do it.' I was still holding the piece of paper between two fingers, like it was an unexploded bomb.

Gav said, 'Thank goodness someone's seen sense.'

'But I can't do it,' I gasped.

'Of course, you can,' Gav said, as he pulled away.

I was sure things couldn't possibly get any worse, until I unfolded the piece of paper to look at the speech. Zandra hadn't even done one. It was just the list of reasons we'd made. And now there was no time for me to write one. I waved the piece of paper in front of Gav.

'What am I gonna do? What am I gonna say?'

'You don't need anyone else to tell you what to say,' he told me. 'Use the list if you need it, but, you know it already. You've done this before. You're getting good at it. Remember, give it a bit of passion. *Un cri de coeur!* He could see by my face that this was no time for French. '*A cry from the heart,*' he explained.

I was so terrified I could hardly speak, never mind cry.

'Cheer up,' said Gav. 'It'll all soon be over.'

Not soon enough, I thought. At that moment I'd have done almost anything to get out of it. I was wishing, as hard as I'd ever wished in my life, that something, anything, might happen to save me. So five minutes later, when Evie broke down, that felt like my fault too.

nineteen

We were just coming into town, when Evie's coughing and spluttering changed to a rattle and a bang. After that it sounded as if we were dragging a string of tin cans behind us.

'Nobody panic,' said Gav. 'It's just the exhaust's fallen off.'

We piled out to look at the damage. Evie had grown a long tail. While Gav decided what to do, we stood back on the grass verge, worrying about whether we were gonna make it in time. Tex was waving his mobile around, offering to ring the AA, but Gav said there was no need for that, did anyone have a skipping rope? We all looked at him as if he'd finally lost it.

'This is no time for keep fit,' said Maxine.

'To tie the exhaust back on,' he explained.

Well, we're a bit past skipping ropes, but guess who saved the day – again? Tex said he had a dog lead in his bag. Goodness knows why, 'cos I'd never seen Chipshop on a lead in his life.

We all had to help push Evie off the road and onto the grass verge. She might have looked like a bit of a rust bucket but even with seven of us pushing it felt like trying to move a mountain.

'Looks like the revolution well and truly broke down,' said Abi.

'At least Zandra'll be able to give the speech,' said Hemma, 'even if we don't get there in time.'

'Yeah. What a good job she went with Miss Summers,' agreed Maxine.

I couldn't keep it in any longer. 'It would be,' I said, 'if she'd taken this with her,' and I waved the list of reasons in front of them.

'What are you doing with that?' they all gasped.

'Zandra says she can't do the speech. She says I've gotta do it.'

'Ooh, err,' said Maxine. 'Better get a move on, Gav.'

Gav slid out from under Evie. 'Relax,' he said. 'They can't start without us; we've got the star player on board.'

'Yeah, Jelly's the star!' the others started chanting.

I tried to smile, but to tell you the truth by now there was only a little bit of me wanted to get there in time, the rest of me was praying, *make us too late, please, make us too late.*

But it didn't work.

When we arrived at the Town Hall there was quite a crowd gathered on the pavement waiting for us.

'There's my dad!' yelled Tex. Tex's dad and his

mates were holding up placards saying: *Hands Off School Sports!* and *Kids Need Competitive Sport!* And Chipshop was there with a little dog-sized sandwich board with the message: *Save Our Netball* on it.

Gav let the others out of the van. For a minute I couldn't move. OK, I thought, this is it, then, the worst day of my life, but I knew I couldn't sit in the van all day, so I made myself climb out too.

The first big surprise was seeing my mum and dad there.

'We thought you'd never get here,' Mum shouted over the crowd. She pushed through and gave me a big hug that was nearly the end of me. She said it had all been Gav's idea. Mrs Barker hadn't wanted to give her the time off, but Mum'd put her foot down. And Dad said he'd manage without his extra beauty sleep. Wasn't he beautiful enough already?

I tried not to start crying and turned to look for Gav but he must've gone to park Evie. I still hadn't given him Deedee's message and I was feeling such a coward about it. Just then Miss Summers raced over and grabbed me. 'Zandra's told me you're going to do the speech. You'll be great, Jelly, I know you will.'

Zandra was standing behind her. She hardly dared to look at me. I think she was scared I might still give her the paper back, but before I got the chance to, we were rounded up by a young woman from the council called Megan.

'Come along, come along. Do you have any idea how late you are? The Committee's waiting. We'll have to run.'

Suddenly we were all racing down these huge wide corridors trying to keep up. I thought I'd been nervous before, but now we were inside the building...it was awesome. Megan took us up a big flight of stairs and down another long corridor with huge paintings on the walls. Then just as we reached the Council Chamber Abi said, 'Excuse me, Miss, but...I really need the loo.'

Everyone laughed, but then they all said, 'Yeah, me too.' So we had to go almost back to where we'd come in. Megan didn't really mind. She said we were probably all feeling nervous. I didn't know why anyone else should be nervous; they didn't have to do anything.

I sat on the loo having a last look at the list of reasons, but then someone tapped on the toilet door.

'Jelly, are you in there?' It was Zandra. When I opened the door her and Alicia pushed inside with me. There was hardly room to move.

'Listen, I'm really sorry,' she said, 'but I couldn't help it. It's not that I don't care about netball. I just don't care about it as much as you do. I was lying on my bed last night thinking, I wish

Jelly was doing this, not me. She'd do it much better.'

I couldn't believe it. 'But why didn't you say anything before?' I asked her.

'I was too scared.'

'You? Scared!'

'Everyone thinks oh, Zandra'll do it! It's easy for her. But nobody ever bothers to ask me. And sometimes I *hate* it.'

Then she started to cry. I didn't know what to do. I wanted to tell her it was OK, I didn't mind doing it, but that would've been a big, fat lie! I did feel sorry for her, though, but before I could put my arm round her Abi was hammering on the toilet door shouting, 'Megan says we've gotta go. Now!'

You should have seen Abi's face when she saw me and Zandra and Alicia coming out of the loo together. Classic.

Before we went in, Megan said, 'There's going to be TV cameras in there, but don't worry, they're not there just because of you. The Chairman's decided to allow them in since it's a matter of public interest.'

As if it wasn't scary enough already, I thought. The next moment Megan led us all inside. Tex gave my arm a squeeze and grinned at me. But I couldn't even smile back. I was wondering if anyone had ever died of fear. I thought, it's not fair. Eleven's far too young to die.

Did I say it was scarier once we got inside the Town Hall? That was nothing. Inside the Council Chamber it felt like *1st League Championship Scary*. In the middle of this huge room there was a big curved table with about ten people round it. I knew they had to be the councillors: Stan Edgar was one of them. And horrible *Pasty the Poisoner* was there. On other tables there were people with notepads and keyboards in front of them, including that smarmy reporter. He even had the nerve to wave at me, as if we were friends! What a cheek!

Mum and Dad waved at me from the public gallery. Gav was back from parking Evie and he was holding up the banner saying: *Vive la Revolution!* I could hardly believe who was there with him: Deedee, waving a big notice that said: *I did it!* So I guessed she'd got the job. But then she turned it over and on the other side it said, *You can do it too!* I might've been wrong, because my head was in such a spin, but I could have sworn she was...holding hands with Gav!

There was a group of chairs set out for us. Megan told me to sit on the end one. She told me when the Chairman called my name I should stand up so everyone could see me. She said she'd warn me a couple of minutes before.

'But you'll be fine,' she said. Easy for her to say!

Miss Summers was sitting next to me, smiling and squeezing my hand. A bit too tight actually. I couldn't feel my fingers any more and I dropped the paper with the list of reasons on the floor. Zandra bent down and picked it up. When she gave it me back she whispered, 'You can do it, Jelly.'

Then I spotted Mrs Barker sitting behind Mum and Dad. I thought if she knew Zandra and me had swopped places she'd come flying down to sort us out. But it was already too late. The place had suddenly gone quiet.

I tried to remember how I'd ended up here, doing the scariest thing in my life, but it all felt mixed up like in a dream. I just wanted to wake up and find out that's all it had been – a big dream.

The Chairman said they were ready to move on to the next item on the agenda. Now it was too late to back out because the next item was me.

twenty

'The next item concerns the council's decision to ban competitive sports in schools,' the Chairman said, 'There are a number of reasons why the Scrutiny Committee has decided to look at this decision. The first is in response to a petition we've received...'

Megan leaned forward and gave me a little nudge. I jumped out of my chair and almost out of my skin.

'Not just yet,' she whispered, pulling me back, 'but get ready.'

I didn't hear the rest of what the Chairman said because the panic had grown and now it was filling my head, like a swarm of bees had set up home in there. Then through the buzzing I suddenly realised I'd heard my name called twice already.

I stood up and took a step forward like I was sleepwalking. It was a long time since I'd felt this small. I held the list out in front of me but my hand was shaking so much I couldn't read a word of it. I could feel everyone staring at me from all over the room. I could see my mum and dad and Gav and Deedee all looking down on me. The stupid newspaper reporter, and the committee, and the rest of the team. And Mrs Barker. She looked as if she couldn't believe her eyes. They were all watching me, wondering if I was going to go on standing there saying nothing, just looking stupid, for ever. I was wondering too.

I don't know how many seconds or minutes it lasted – it felt like hours to me. All the while *Pasty the Poisoner* was smiling her smarmy smile at me. I tell you, I almost sat down again. But then I saw Stan Edgar wink at me. And Tex leaned forward and whispered, 'Go Jelly. Go for it! *You're a star!*

So I took a couple of deep breaths and then...took a shot.

'OK,' I said. 'I admit when I said you were a load of loonies – it wasn't clever. And it wasn't what I meant. But...we couldn't understand why anybody in their right mind would want to ban netball in the first place. Nobody's given us one good reason so far. Well, we've got a long list of reasons against it.' And I waved the list to show them.

I went through them all, counting them off on my fingers. Gav was right, I did know it already, I didn't really need the list to remind me. When I came to the last reason, I looked round at the rest of my team, all cheering me on, and I was glad I'd saved the main reason till last: *It's good to be part of a team.*

'Being in a team's like having another family,' I said. 'Yeah, you have your squabbles, but it's like you belong together.' I looked up at Deedee and she jumped to her feet and called out, 'Right on, sister!' Everybody laughed at that.

'You don't always have to like each other,' I carried on. 'But you still pull together if you want to win. You can always rely on your team never to let you down even if it's not always easy.'

I told them how Maxine sometimes has to beg her next door neighbour to look after her kid brothers so she can get to practices and Hemma can't come at all unless she drags her sister Nila with her. And Zandra and Alicia, well, they gave up their dancing, when it mattered.

'When you're playing a sport,' I said, 'winning feels like the most important thing in the world, and that's a fantastic feeling. But it's not just about winning. It's doing something you love, something you're good at, and doing it together. That's *magic.*

'Of course everybody can't be good at sport. You'd have to be...' I thought, choose your words carefully here, girl, '*a bit dim* to think that. You can't make us all the same, 'cos we're not, but who cares? Everyone's good at something: dancing, chess, art, *maths even*. But nobody's banning maths, even though we can't all be good at that either.

'I don't want the brainboxes pretending they're thick, just to make me feel better,' I said, 'where's the point in that? Before netball, I used to think I was stupid, 'cos there wasn't anything I was any good at. But netball's made me realise there *is* something – one thing I'm really good at. It makes me feel like a star! And nobody has any right to take it off me!'

Now I was on a roll. 'You should be finding out what different kinds of magic people've got inside them, not trying to make us all the same. 'Cos I think, the more different we are the better.' I looked up at Gav and he waved his fist at me to let me know I was doing fine. 'I've got a friend,' I said. 'He's pretty smart, most of the time. Sometimes he talks a bit weird; sometimes he talks French. This is a bit he taught me the other day...' And I just stuck my arm in the air, like Gav does, clenched my fist and let out an almighty shout: '*VIVE LA DIFFERENCE!*

And then I listened to my voice echoing round that great big room on its own and it sounded sooo...stupid I nearly died. No one joined in or made a sound. OK, I hadn't died of fear, but I might still die of embarrassment. I reckoned I was about to find out.

twenty-one

Time seemed to be playing tricks again. It felt like minutes before anyone else made a sound. But then it came in a great big wave. Like we were playing in the final of the league and I'd just scored the winning goal. The whole place went *bananas*.

Everyone in the public gallery was on their feet, cheering and whistling. The rest of the team were chanting: *Vive La Difference!* Lots of the councillors were clapping. Stan Edgar stood up and bowed to me, like I was the Queen or something. I was so embarrassed, but I couldn't help smiling. I knew then it had to be him that had got us the invitation. For once even Mrs Barker didn't look like she wanted to shut me up.

The only person who didn't look happy was *Pasty the Poisoner*. She stared at me and this time I stared right back. I remembered what Gav had said about even adults feeling frightened and for a second that's how she looked. Then she was hammering on the table in front of her, shouting, 'I insist the room is cleared unless this rowdy behaviour ceases immediately.'

The noise started to die down so everyone heard the Chairman say, 'Mrs Poysner may like to remember that on this occasion she's not in the chair. However, we do still have a lot of business to get through, so I'd like to thank Miss Jackson (nobody's ever called me that before!) and her team for coming. She spoke clearly and with passion. We'll give all her arguments our full consideration after Mrs Poysner has had a chance to reply and Councillor Edgar has spoken on the wider implications for the sale of school playing fields *if* this ban were to be approved.'

Megan led us all out then. The rest of the team was as excited as if they'd done the speech themselves.

'You were really brilliant, Jelly,' Zandra said. 'I couldn't have done it as well as that.'

Maxine said the best bit was *Pasty the Poisoner's* face. 'She looked as if she'd eaten something disgusting,' she laughed.

Everyone went quiet then 'cos Mrs Barker suddenly appeared.

'Well, Angelina, what a surprise,' she said. 'Who would have thought you were capable of that performance?' She even smiled at me!

I asked Miss Summers what she thought would happen next. She said, 'There'll be a bit more discussion and then they'll move to a vote. But whatever the decision, Jelly, you couldn't have done any better.'

I couldn't believe we'd got to wait even longer to find out the result. It's a good job they don't organise netball matches like that.

While we waited, Mum and Dad and some of the other parents came to join us. Tex was acting a bit weird. He kept saying: *Jelly for Prime Minister* and silly things like that. And hugging my arm. There was a bit too much hugging for my liking.

Gav told me, 'That was quite a performance. Full of passion, but right to the point. You see, Jelly, netball's not your only bit of magic.'

'I've been telling her that,' Tex agreed.

'Anyway it's all thanks to you,' I told Gav.

'For what?' he said. 'You did it all yourself.'

'For the chats, the lifts – the French even. Everything,' I said.

'My pleasure, *mon ami*.'

Even our Deedee gave me a hug and said, 'I never knew you had it in you, kiddo.'

You could tell by the way she and Gav were grinning and looking all pink that something was definitely going on. The minute she went to get a drink, I asked him, 'So, what's the story with you two?'

Gav told me that when he'd gone to pick Deedee up to take her to her interview she'd given him another earful. She'd told him it was time to choose. But Gav had said that he already had. He'd chosen to keep his promise to me, but, as far as whose boyfriend he wanted to be, there was no competition. And he was gonna take her to see a film tonight. Then they'd go for a pizza to celebrate the new job that she was bound to get. Deedee still hadn't said anything. So Gav had pressed her, 'That's a date then?'

Deedee hadn't been keen on calling it *a date*, exactly. But Gav had said, 'A date's a date, as far as I'm concerned and whatever you call it, Deedee, that's what's on offer. Take it or leave it.'

Wow! I thought, Way to go, Gav!

'So thanks to you too, Jelly,' Gav said.

'For what?' I asked him.

'For the chats, the advice – everything.'

'My pleasure, *mon ami*,' I told him.

Just then a message came down for us to go back into the Council Chamber. This is it, I thought. After everything we'd been through I just couldn't bear to hear we'd lost.

On the way back into the Chamber Tex's dad told us there was a bit more going on than just banning our netball. He said there was a lot of money involved, because it would very likely lead to lots of schools selling off their playing fields. He said our petition had given the committee an excuse to investigate a bit further.

'So do you think we've won?' I asked him.

'Ah, well, that's another matter,' he said. 'But we'll soon find out.'

We went in and sat down. The Chairman began to explain that now they'd had a chance to discuss and hear each other's points of view they'd finally voted. He didn't want to keep us in suspense a moment longer than was necessary but he had to tell us that the outcome of the vote had been close, very close indeed....

I thought words, words, words, why can't he just say yes or—

Suddenly there was an almighty cheer and everyone was on their feet. We'd won. We'd WON! It might have sounded before like we'd won the league, now it sounded like we'd won the World Cup. And everyone there seemed to be on our side.

Well, *nearly* everyone. *Pasty the Poisoner's* face was all screwed up and her big bulgy eyes looked as if they couldn't believe what they were seeing. She banged her fist on the table, like a three-year-old, shouting, '*This is not fair!*

Gradually everyone stopped cheering and turned to look at her. She tried to calm herself down, but she didn't do very well. She pointed at us and shouted, 'You haven't heard the end of this. This was my bill and *no one's* taking it away from me.' Then she grabbed her papers off the table, stamped her foot and stormed out of the Chamber. Result!

Before we left, Stan Edgar came out to have a word with us. He shook my hand and said I'd done very well and one day I'd make a real politician. I was glad no one else heard. I felt daft enough already.

On the way home I sat in the back of the van with the others 'cos Deedee was in the front with Gav, whispering in his ear. Oh, yuk! Then even Tex went all soft on me. He only asked me to be his girlfriend! P-lease. Like I told him, he only comes up to my elbow.

'So what?' he said. '*Vive la difference!*'

I had to put him in a headlock then, till he swore he was only kidding. But don't worry, he soon got his priorities right. All through the Easter holidays and every night after school for the past two weeks he's been helping me practise. He's still my best buddy, after all.

And today's the big day: the County Netball League Final.

Everybody's here: the rest of the team, all their mums and dads, Miss Summers, my whole family and good old Gav, of course, Stan Edgar and his wife, even Mrs Barker's here – *everyone*. They've all come to see me and my team win. Yeah, I did say *my* team. Miss Summers made Zandra and me joint captains. It was Zandra's idea.

And I did say win, too. I know, you're thinking, didn't she say at the start : don't count your goals till they're in the net? So what if I did. They don't call me the *Shooting Star* for nothing and it's not like I've gotta give a speech or something difficult. I know I can do this. *This* is my little bit of magic. And no one's taking it away from me. No way!

Orchard Red Apples

My Scary Fairy Godmother	Rose Impey	1 84362 683 7
The Truth Cookie	Fiona Dunbar	1 84362 549 0
Cupid Cakes	Fiona Dunbar	1 84362 688 8
Chocolate Wishes	Fiona Dunbar	1 84362 689 6
Utterly Me, Clarice Bean	Lauren Child	1 84362 304 8
Clarice Bean Spells Trouble	Lauren Child	1 84362 858 9
The Fire Within	Chris d'Lacey	1 84121 533 3
IceFire	Chris d'Lacey	1 84362 373 0
You're Amazing Mr Jupiter	Sue Limb	1 84362 614 4
Shadowmaster	Andrew Mathews	1 84362 187 8
The Time of the Stars	Andrew Matthews	1 84362 189 4
The Darkening	Andrew Matthews	1 84362 188 6
Do Not Read This Book	Pat Moon	1 84121 435 3
Do Not Read Any Further	Pat Moon	1 84121 456 6
Tower-block Pony	Alison Prince	1 84362 648 9

All priced at £4.99